PRINCESS OF BABYLON

PALACE OF THE ORNAMENTS
BOOK ONE

KYLIE QUILLINAN

CHAPTER 1

"Princess! Quick! Father!"

Tall's voice echoed down the stone hallway. My tutor stopped mid-speech and glared down his nose at me.

"It would seem Father has summoned me," I said.

I rose from my cushion on the stone floor, inelegant as my sandals tangled in my tunic, sending me pitching forward into my tutor's arms. He thrust me back away from him, swift to move lest anyone see me in his embrace and came to the wrong conclusion. Tall's voice retreated down the hallway as he passed our chamber.

"Tall," I called after him. "I am here."

He ran back to me.

"Quick!" He flapped his hands near his face to express the urgency of the summons. "Chaos! Uproar!"

"Come on then," I said. "You can tell me on the way."

"Father!" he said, trotting beside me as I strode down the hallway.

If he had any other name, Tall had long forgotten it. Most people regarded him as a simpleton and he was often the butt of jokes, but to me it seemed his mind was no less sharp than mine.

1

He just didn't have the ability to express his thoughts in anything more than single words. However, once I became accustomed to his manner of speaking, I found I could understand him perfectly well.

"Do you know why Father has summoned me?" I asked.

His hands flapped again, the thing he always did when he was anxious.

"Uproar! Sister!"

"Oh dear, is she injured?"

"Disaster!"

My older sister, Ishtar, was the perfect daughter. The beautiful one. The one who walked elegantly and sang sweetly and always had a witty comment ready. Our father thought she was practically the incarnation of the goddess Ishtar for whom she was named, she was so lovely. I, on the other hand, was clumsy and graceless, my face was plain, I couldn't sing to save my life, and I was more interested in learning about history and politics than trading clever banter with potential suitors. I was a constant disappointment to our father who had hoped for two perfect daughters to marry off.

Although Ishtar was only fifteen years old, Father had already arranged a marriage for her. Tomorrow she would leave for Egypt, sailing away with a flotilla of ships bearing gifts for her intended husband. She was to marry Pharaoh and be his queen. Any excitement I might have felt for her was marred by my sadness at knowing I would never see her again.

As for me, our father had yet to negotiate a suitable marriage, even though I was only a year younger than Ishtar. It seemed no man wanted me for his wife, although I was a princess and daughter of the Great and Mighty Marduk-apla-iddina of Babylon.

We reached Father's audience chamber and Tall stopped at the door, his hands flapping.

"Here!" he said.

"It is all right. You don't have to come in with me."

"Safe!"

"Yes, yes, I will be perfectly safe."

Sometimes Tall couldn't find the right word to express himself. I doubted he thought I would be in danger within Father's audience chamber, but perhaps he thought I would be afraid without him. Whatever had happened must be dire indeed.

"Wait here for me." I patted his arm, checked my tunic hung neatly, and entered the chamber.

Even if Tall hadn't warned me, I would have known something was wrong. There were fewer people in here than usual, just Father's personal guards who surrounded his throne as always, his most favoured administrator, and a handful of servants. There were no other administrators or scribes, messenger boys or folk who had brought a case for Father's adjudication.

Ishtar knelt in front of Father, her forehead pressed to the mosaic tiles. Her shoulders shook as she sobbed. Father sat with his arms crossed and a look of distinct displeasure on his face. Even in his aggravation, he still sat with his back straight and his head high. His curly black beard was immaculately groomed as always. Anyone who saw him would know he was an important man, even if they didn't recognise him as their king. Father's gaze shot straight to me.

"Kassaya," he said. "You took your time."

"Father, I apologise if I kept you waiting. I was at a lesson with my tutor. I came as soon as Tall found me."

I knelt and pressed my forehead to the floor like Ishtar. The tiles were cool and smooth, variegated shades of purple which spread out like a sun from Father's throne.

"I sent twelve servants in search of you," Father said. "Why is it always the idiot who is the only one able to locate you?"

I said nothing. I knew Father well enough to know the words

were more observation than question. Beside me, Ishtar still sobbed quietly.

"Kassaya, you may rise," Father said.

I held my tunic away from my sandals as I got to my feet. Father did not seem to be in a mood that would tolerate me tripping and sprawling in front of his throne. Ishtar stayed where she was, her forehead pressed to the floor. She would not dare to rise until Father bid her.

"As you know," Father said, "your sister was supposed to depart for Egypt tomorrow."

I glanced down at Ishtar's shaking shoulders. *Supposed* to depart? Had Pharaoh changed his mind about taking a princess of Babylon as his queen? Had he died or fallen grievously ill?

"Your sister, it seems, had no intention of obeying my wishes," Father said.

I blinked in surprise, but managed to keep my mouth shut. This was not the time for questions. Father would tell me what had happened, or he wouldn't and I would get it out of Ishtar later.

"She has gone and gotten herself with child." Father's voice was cold.

Ishtar had a secret lover? Why would she risk the alliance with Egypt for a dalliance with a man she would never see again and who would likely forget her as soon as she sailed away? A chill washed over me as I realised the implication for myself.

Father could hardly send a pregnant bride to Pharaoh.

Nor would he risk offending Babylon's most powerful ally by breaking an agreement already made.

If Ishtar could not go to Egypt, another daughter of Marduk-apla-iddina would be sent in her place.

Marduk-apla-iddina had five sons, but he had only one other daughter.

Me.

CHAPTER 2

"You depart at dawn," Father said. "Go prepare yourself. The maids who were intended to accompany your sister will go with you. My administrator will attend you in your bedchamber shortly to receive a list of anyone else you wish to take. All other arrangements remain unchanged."

Ishtar sobbed even harder. The loss of her favourite maids would be a bitter blow to her. She had personally selected each of the women who attended to her and sometimes I felt she loved them better than she loved me.

I swallowed down my dismay and bowed low, then left before any unwise words could escape my mouth. Father was not the sort of man one argued with. Once he had made a proclamation — whatever it was — obedience was the only option.

Tall was gone when I exited the audience chamber. Perhaps a guard found him lingering in the hallway and chased him away. I hurried to my bedchamber, seeing nothing of the long hallways lined with potted plants, their walls tastefully decorated with frescoes from the finest artists. I reached my chamber just in time to close the door before a tear rolled down my cheeks. I scrubbed it away and sniffled. I would not cry. Father hadn't raised me to snivel. This was what he required of me and I would do my duty with my head held high. I, Kassaya, daughter of Marduk-apla-iddina, would sail to Egypt and marry Pharaoh. I would be his queen.

The door opened and my mother slipped inside.

"Kassaya," she said and held out her arms to me.

My resolve not to cry crumbled and I flung myself into her arms. I would never see my mother again. Egypt was a long way from Babylon and even if Pharaoh took me with him when he travelled to war, it was unlikely I would ever come here. After all, my marriage was intended to prevent any possibility of war with the Egyptians. I was the payment to strengthen our alliance. The sacrifice of my happiness would be of little consequence in Father's opinion.

As my tears abated, Mother brushed a hair from my cheek. She was as composed as ever. Always the perfect queen, Mother wouldn't shed a tear of regret over one of Father's rulings, even in private.

"I expected to lose a daughter tomorrow," she said. "I suppose it hardly matters which one it is."

My tears returned at her words.

"You must do your father proud, my child," Mother said. "Show Pharaoh what the women of Babylon are made of. Do not cry or plead or disobey him. Give him as many sons as you can and do it with a smile on your face. Show Pharaoh that Babylon is a strong and worthy ally. And always remember, dear child, that one day a son of a princess of Babylon will be Pharaoh of Egypt."

"Yes, Mother."

I could hardly ask what she knew about Ishtar's pregnancy after such a speech. Surely Ishtar hadn't meant to disobey Father. Surely her pregnancy was an accident.

Mother patted my cheek and smiled at me.

"Farewell, Daughter," she said.

She left quickly, but not before I saw her eyes fill with tears. So it seemed Mother did cry, even if she pretended to be unbothered by Father's decision.

The door closed and my tears came again. I hastily wiped them away in case Mother came back. *Show Pharaoh that Babylon is a strong and worthy ally,* she had said. And I would be queen. That was something I never expected. It was always Ishtar who was supposed to be queen of somewhere. We both grew up knowing that as the oldest and prettiest daughter, she would make the most favourable marriage. But now she would stay here in Babylon and it was me who would travel over the seas to be a queen.

I went to the window and looked out at the view I would never again see. Dur-Kurigalzu — my father's stronghold — sprawled before me. Beyond that lay Babylon. To my right, just visible at the edge of my window, stood the Great Temple, its stepped sides rising high into the sky, casting welcome shade over the buildings that crouched at its base. Over it all stretched an endless blue sky, the sun a fierce ball of flame that teased the horizon. A gentle breeze kissed my cheeks, drying the tears I hadn't noticed were falling again. Babylon, city of my birth, and the place I had never thought to leave. A knock sounded on the door and I wiped my eyes.

"Enter," I called.

The door opened and Father's administrator came in, followed by two scribes. The administrator was a short, stocky man with a black beard that fell to halfway down his chest. He gave me a brief bow, then gestured for the scribes to set up their writing stations. The two men dropped to their knees and positioned their little wooden tables in front of them, on which they set reed styluses and fresh blocks of wet clay.

"Your Father instructs you to name those you wish to accompany you," the administrator said.

He waited, clearly expecting me to have already decided. My mind whirled. This decision needed careful thought, but I couldn't send the man back to Father without the list he expected.

"Tall," I said. I was his only friend and without me, he would endure nothing but scorn and mockery. "Also Half."

Half was so named because he stood barely half as high as a man. Folk in the palace were cruel to those who were different. Some called him Halfwit and joked they would need two of him to make a whole man, even though like Tall, Half's mind was as sharp as anyone's. I wondered sometimes what folk said of me behind my back, given my tendency to befriend those who were considered outcasts.

"Your tutor?" the administrator asked as the scribes pressed their reeds into the soft clay to make the necessary cuneiform symbols to record my words.

I hesitated. The man was a valuable source of information about politics, history and geography, but he was also scathing towards both Tall and Half. The people I took with me should be those who would be allies. Friends in a foreign land. I could not see my tutor becoming my friend.

"No," I said. "But find me someone who speaks Egyptian and who is knowledgable in their history and customs. A woman if possible."

Ishtar had been tutored in the Egyptian language far more extensively than I had. I supposed Father had long planned her grand marriage would be to Pharaoh. I could greet an Egyptian in their own speech and if they spoke slowly enough I could understand some of what they said. But if I was to be queen, I needed fluency in their language and I wanted to understand the people I would rule over. I would pass the weeks of the journey to Egypt by learning everything I could.

"Do you wish any of your maids to accompany you?" the

administrator asked. "Your father suggests they transfer to your sister since hers will be travelling with you."

From the way he worded it, I understood Father had already made the decision.

"That will be satisfactory," I said.

I wouldn't be sorry to leave behind those chattering gossips. I fled their intrusion as much as possible, dressing myself early before they arrived and pretending I had lessons even when I didn't to give me a reason to escape them. Ishtar's maids would be no better, but perhaps customs would be different in Egypt. Perhaps I would not be expected to tolerate a contingent of women who had nothing to do other than fix my face, arrange my hair, and gossip about everything they saw. Once I was queen, I wouldn't have time for such things anyway.

The administrator waited, clearly expecting me to name others. What would Father do if I requested Ishtar to accompany me? Since it was supposed to be she who went, why shouldn't I ask for her? She could be the one to teach me Egyptian. But antagonising Father now, just before I left forever, served no point.

Should I request guards? No, Father would send a squadron, at least, with me. He wouldn't send his daughter all the way across the sea without men to protect her.

"That will be sufficient," I said.

The administrator barely concealed his surprise as he bowed and left. How many people had he expected me to name? Other than Tall and Half, there was nobody else I considered a friend. There were plenty of girls my age around the palace while I was growing up, but they were always too aware that I was a princess and they weren't. I never had a chance to grow close to any of them and it never bothered me since I had Ishtar as both sister and friend. Only it seemed I didn't know her as well as I thought.

Ishtar's three maids arrived shortly afterwards, sent to help pack my things. They were of little use, too busy sobbing and seemingly gasping for air with the shock of being parted from their beloved mistress. I ignored their hysterics and packed those things I couldn't bear to leave behind: a few favourite jewels, my hairbrush with the handle carved from the ivory of a beast I had been told was almost as big as the Great Temple, a delicate creamy coloured shell brought from Syria by my Father when I was a child, and a scarf embroidered for me by Ishtar. Her needlework was exquisite and far finer than mine. I tried, but my stitches were never straight and the fabric always sat unevenly.

That was everything which was precious to me. Everything that would cause me sorrow to be parted from. I supposed when I was queen whatever I needed would be provided for me, but these small treasures would remind me of where I came from.

Ishtar slipped into my chamber later that evening as I lay sleepless. She climbed into my bed and curled up against my back, just like she used to when we were children. Her body shook as she sobbed.

"Sister, I am sorry," she said. "But I couldn't bear to go."

"Who is the father?" My voice was colder than I intended, but it was too late to take back the words. "Do you love him?"

"He was a means to an end."

I pulled away and sat up so I could face her.

"You deliberately got yourself with child?"

Surely I had misunderstood. She was supposed to be queen. Most girls would give their left hand for such an opportunity. Not me, though. To me, it seemed a fate little worse than death.

Ishtar sobbed harder.

"I couldn't do it," she said when her tears abated. In the moonlight streaming through my open window, I could see her perfect face was swollen from crying. It hardly marred her beauty. "To leave Babylon and know I would never return? To leave everything and everyone I have ever known?"

"Your maids were to go with you."

"But I would never see Mother again, or Father. Or you."

Was I truly her last thought? We were sisters. I had always thought we loved each other. But she contrived a scheme to get herself released, knowing it was me who would have to go.

"And now it is I who will never return to Babylon," I said. "And you will still never see me again."

I didn't try to hide the bitterness in my voice. She had done this deliberately. Trapped me in a life she knew I never wanted. I would have been perfectly happy to spend the rest of my life in Father's palace, married to whichever noble man he chose for me, and passing my days here in Babylon, with access to the finest tutors and archives in the world and all the wisdom people had ever known. How much I could have learned with all the years that were ahead of me. Now I would be queen and would likely never have time to learn anything ever again.

Ishtar sobbed grievously at my displeasure and I was too angry to soothe her.

"You should return to your own chamber," I said. "I need to sleep. I have a long journey tomorrow."

As the door closed quietly behind her, I knew I would never see my sister again.

CHAPTER 3

$\mathcal{I}$ was woken at dawn the next day when the administrator bustled into my chamber, followed by Ishtar's three maids and a full dozen servants. While the maids made up my face and arranged my hair, the administrator inspected each item in my chamber and directed the servants as to what was to be taken to the ships.

I studied my chamber as the maids worked on me, trying to see it with the administrator's eyes. Someone had opened the wooden shutters to let in the light and the air, which was still fresh in these early hours before the humidity set in. Fine tapestries on the walls and thick rugs for my feet. A low bed draped with netting to keep the insects off me at night. Several chests for my clothes, a stool to sit on while maids attended to me. The furniture was unchanged from my childhood and a little battered now, but it was well made.

Despite the the fineness of my furniture, there was little the administrator deemed worthy of being sent with me, not even most of my clothing. He did instruct the servants to take the small chest I had packed myself, although he frowned hard at me for asking. He finished far too soon to have fairly evaluated my possessions. The servants scurried after him as he left and I was finally alone with the three maids.

The women Ishtar chose to attend her all looked much alike and I could barely tell one from another. I didn't know what any of their birth names were. It amused my sister, who was named for a goddess herself, to call her maids by the names of other goddesses. So every woman who served her was swiftly given a new name and forbidden from ever using her old name again.

They dressed me in an elaborate purple tunic I had never seen before. I presumed it had been made for Ishtar, probably worked on by a team of sewers for the last several months to have it ready for her departure. Made to Ishtar's measurements, it was a little too big in the chest and too short at the hem. The maids clucked and tutted at that, but there was no time for any adjustments.

At last I was ready, with my face painted to their satisfaction and my hair pinned up on my head, threaded with silver bells and golden beads. It all took much longer than it should have since they frequently had to stop and compose themselves.

"Do you have any possessions of your own you wish to bring?" I asked them.

All three began sobbing again. At length, one of them managed to speak.

"We were permitted to take one chest each. Our things were already sent to the ships yesterday. Before we knew."

She collapsed into tears again. One of the others wrapped her arms around her and they cried on each other's shoulders. I barely managed to restrain my sigh. Please Marduk, don't let them cry like this all the way to Egypt.

"I suppose it is time to leave then," I said.

Too busy with their sobbing, none of the women even acknowledged me.

"That is enough," I said. "Dry your tears. You are supposed to attend me and you cannot do that if you spend all day crying.

Remember, you are women of Babylon. Subjects of the Great and Mighty Marduk-apla-iddina. It is time you acted like it."

Two of the women gaped at me. Clearly Ishtar had never spoken so sternly to them. But the third dried her tears with her sleeve and straightened her shoulders.

"Of course, Princess." Her voice wobbled, but at least she was trying. "If you are ready to leave, transport awaits you at the main entrance."

"Let's go then."

With one last look around the chamber that had been mine ever since I was old enough to move out of the nursery, I left. My fingers touched the doorframe as I passed through it, lingering on the hip-height notch, a memory of childhood clumsiness. The three women followed me, two still sobbing.

"You heard her," the same woman said. "Wipe away your tears. We are women of Babylon and the personal maids of the future Queen of Egypt."

I cast a glance at her over my shoulder.

"What is your name?" I asked.

"Tiamat, Princess."

Tiamat, at least, I should be able to tell apart from the others, or I could as long as she was the only one not crying. The other two still struggled to get their sobs under control. I shot them each a sharp look and they swiftly wiped away their tears. With my head held high, I made my way to the main entrance.

I heard the noise long before I reached the doors, even though they still stood closed. Shouting and cheering almost drowned out the lutes, pipes and drums.

"What in Marduk's name is going on out there?" I spoke to myself and didn't expect any of the women to have an answer.

"A parade, Princess," Tiamat said. "In your honour. They are to escort you to the ships."

I closed my eyes for a moment, preparing myself. I should have known my escort wouldn't be merely a few guards and my newly acquired maids. As the doors opened, the noise deafened me.

Folk filled the entire street outside. Musicians and dancers performed for the crowd's entertainment. Enterprising cooks had set up makeshift stalls along the side of the road and the aroma of roasting meats and fresh bread made my stomach growl. A great cry rose from the crowd as they spotted me standing at the doors. From behind me came Tiamat's voice.

"Well, I suppose there is nothing to be done but to keep moving forward," she said.

I took a deep breath and straightened my shoulders. I was a Princess of Babylon, and I would make my king proud.

I raised my hand in acknowledgement and the crowd roared. Did they know it was Ishtar who was supposed to depart today, or did one daughter of Marduk-apla-iddina look much like another to them? With another deep breath, I squared my shoulders, held up my tunic a little so I wouldn't trip, and very carefully descended the steps. A pair of palanquin waited, each with a full dozen slaves to bear them. I supposed one was for me and the other for my maids. It was only when I reached the bottom that I saw my father.

His throne was set on a raised platform off to the side of the steps. I lowered myself to kneel before him, my tunic protected by the rug that had been placed there for precisely this purpose. I pressed my forehead to the ground and waited. The crowd quietened, although folk still shuffled their feet as they tried to secure a better view. Children whispered, a baby cried. Somewhere further away, a dog barked, a rooster crowed.

"Rise, Kassaya, Princess of Babylon." My father's voice was formal, giving no hint of how he felt at farewelling his youngest daughter.

I got up slowly, careful not to trip on my hem. Today, of all days, I would not embarrass myself.

"Today we farewell our daughter." My father's voice was

pitched to carry and the crowd quietened as they strained to hear. "It gives us great pride to know our daughter will marry Pharaoh. We bid you to be an obedient wife and to give Pharaoh many sons. We instruct you to always advocate for the benefit of Babylon and to ensure our alliance with Egypt grows ever stronger. We send you to our best and most favoured ally, and we expect you to always be a shining example of a Babylonian woman."

Beside Father's dais, scribes recorded his words on their clay tablets. A copy of Father's speech would be sent with me to be presented to Pharaoh. Other copies would be deposited in the archives, safeguarded for all prosperity so the generations who followed would know what Marduk-apla-iddina said as he sent his youngest daughter to Egypt.

I bowed low from my waist and touched my fingers to my lips as a sign of respect for my king. I didn't speak. Marduk-apla-iddina expected no response from me. He expected only obedience.

CHAPTER 4

*O*nce Father had said everything he intended to, he rose from his throne and left. There were no private farewells for the daughter he would never see again.

"Princess," a guard said to me. "Are you ready?"

I scanned the palanquins. The slaves who stood ready to carry them. The squadron of guards who would surround me as I was transported to the ships. The waiting crowd, which had again begun cheering in anticipation of my departure. No, I wasn't ready. This wasn't supposed to be for me. Mother's words echoed through my mind — *show Pharaoh what the women of Babylon are made of* — and I squared my shoulders. I would show everyone what our women were made of.

"I'm ready," I said to the guard, and if my voice wobbled just the tiniest bit, I doubted he heard it over the cacophony.

He led me to the first palanquin and held my hand as I stepped in. I settled myself on the cushions.

"Are you comfortable, Princess?" the guard asked.

"Well enough."

"Which of your maids do you wish to travel with you?"

I would have preferred to be alone, but I supposed this was my fate now. Perhaps I would never have another moment alone again as long as I lived.

"Tiamat may accompany me." The other two could use the time to get their emotions under control.

The guard beckoned to Tiamat — was I the only one who didn't know each of my sister's maids? — and she came to sit beside me. The slaves raised the palanquin up on their shoulders and we set off. I clenched my hands in my lap and tried to pretend I was at ease. Beside me, Tiamat was silent, although it didn't last for long.

"I suppose this is all very unexpected for you," she observed eventually.

I debated how to answer.

"Did you know about my sister's lover?" I asked.

"No, I was not as close to her as others were."

"So there were those of her maids who knew?"

She hesitated and when I looked over at her, she was biting her lip.

"Were there?" I asked.

"I can't say," she said and I had to lean closer to hear her over the cries from the crowd that lined the street. "If anyone knew, it would have been Nammu. She and Ishtar are as close as sisters. Neither Belet-ili nor I are as dear to her."

I looked out over the crowd, although I saw none of their faces. Tiamat didn't mean to hurt me with her words. She wouldn't know how it wounded me to hear someone else was so close to Ishtar. That Ishtar had shared confidences with a servant and not with me.

"But even had I known, I would not have told anyone," Tiamat said. "You must understand. She was my mistress. If I displeased her in any way, I would lose my position."

"Is that why Nammu said nothing?"

There was a long pause before she replied.

"I don't know," she said. "Her relationship with Ishtar is different to mine."

"Tell me about Nammu and Belet-ili. What should I know about them if they are to serve me?"

"Nammu is most unhappy about being parted from Ishtar," Tiamat said. "And she is a vengeful sort. She may seek to make trouble over it."

"What sort of trouble?"

She shrugged. "Gossip probably. Spreading rumours. Maybe I am wrong, but I don't trust her. She is too much like Ishtar."

I had never heard anyone criticise my sister before. It seemed there was a side to her I hadn't known.

"And Belet-ili?" I asked.

"She is quieter than Nammu, but she will go along with whatever the strongest personality dictates. If Nammu is inclined to trouble, Belet-ili will follow her."

So I potentially had two treacherous snakes in my personal entourage.

"And you?" I asked. "Are you inclined to trouble as well?"

"No, Princess," she said quickly. "I took this position because both my parents are dead and I have no husband. My older sister's husband did what he could for me, but he could barely provide for his own family let alone me as well. I didn't want them to be destitute because of me. If I have work, and perhaps a fair mistress, that is all I desire. I have no interest in spreading gossip or rumours."

"Very good," I said. "I think you and I will get along just fine."

We passed the rest of the journey in silence. The noise made talking difficult anyway. The musicians and acrobats proceeded ahead of us and folk lined both sides of the street all the way to the wharf where six ships awaited our arrival. Sailors swarmed their decks, presumably making their final preparations.

We would travel on one of the ships — me and my personal attendants — while the others would carry the riches sent as my dowry. Gold, silver and gems. Cows, sheep and goats. Rolls of linen and woollen cloth. Anything of great value that could be carried to the ships. These would be sent to Pharaoh, along with Babylon's finest tribute: its princess.

CHAPTER 5

When we reached the docks, the slaves lowered the palanquin to the ground and a guard offered his hand to help me out. I went to straighten my tunic, but Tiamat stopped me with a click of her tongue.

"I should do that for you, Princess," she said. "It is not seemly for you to be seen arranging your own clothing."

I swallowed my retort and allowed her to adjust my tunic. My impending marriage didn't suddenly make me unable to do such a thing for myself, but I supposed I would have to get used to it. I had been accustomed to a great deal of freedom from my maids, a situation which suited both them and me, but I couldn't expect that to continue if I was to be queen.

Behind us, Nammu and Belet-ili disembarked their palanquin. They stood together, talking quietly. When Tiamat cleared her throat loudly and shot them a look, they came to crowd around me, straightening my sleeves and adjusting my hair.

"That is enough." I ducked away from their grasping hands. "I'm sure I look no different than I did an hour ago."

"Your hair was all windblown," one of the women said.

"And your makeup needs to be touched up," the other said. "You wish to look your best for your departure."

Privately, I didn't particularly care. The only people who would be close enough to see such details were the same ones who would sail with us. And they would surely see me in more disarray than this over the duration of our sea voyage.

"Which one are you?" I asked the woman whose fingers again tugged on my sleeve.

"Belet-ili, Princess," she said.

"Stand still and let me look at you."

Her thin face and long dark hair looked much the same as those of Tiamat and Nammu. All three were of a height and each had high cheekbones, an elegantly shaped nose, and long, dark hair pinned up behind their heads. Why in Marduk's name did Ishtar insist on appointing women who all looked alike? Even their tunics were similar, woollen shifts which ended at their knees in bright fringes.

Tiamat's nose was a little smaller than those of the other two women and her eyes were slightly more slanted. She was also the only one who didn't look at me haughtily. She, at least, I could distinguish. Nammu's face was skinnier than Belet-ili's and she was just the tiniest bit taller. As long as I looked carefully, I should be able to tell which was which. A guard appeared at my side, halting my inspection of the women.

"Princess, the ships are ready to depart," he said.

Nammu's face crumpled and I glared at her before she could start crying. She sniffled and at least tried to compose herself. As I followed the guard to the ship, someone behind me let out a sob. I didn't look back to see who it was.

"Where are Tall and Half?" I asked the guard.

"Tall is onboard, but I haven't seen Halfwit," he said.

I shot him a glare.

"His name is Half," I said.

The guard shrugged and didn't look terribly apologetic. There was no point in chastising him further. He and Half would never meet again after today.

I would have known which ship I was to travel on, even if it wasn't the one still at the dock. Its mask was wound with bright ribbons — gold, silver and purple. More ribbons hung from its sides to give it a festive appearance as we set sail.

The other ships waited a little further along the Purattu, the river that stretched the length of Babylon and beyond. Surely Egypt had no river that could compare to the Purattu. My heart ached as I realised this would be the last time I ever sailed our mighty river. I learnt to swim in it, but never again would its warm waters caress my skin. Never again would I sit on its banks and watch the birds and insects drawn to its water. Never again would I eat fish retrieved from its depths.

The guard held my hand to steady me as I ascended the bridge. My new maids followed me, although no guard offered his hand to them. On the deck, the crew secured sails and coiled ropes, stowed away the last of the chests, and completed all manner of other tasks. The captain waited to greet me, a tall man with a curly, black beard. I met his eyes and he gave me a short bow.

"We are almost ready for departure, Princess." His tone was respectful, although his gaze barely left his crew even as he spoke to me.

My throat felt full and I only nodded, uncertain I could trust my voice. *You are a Princess of Babylon,* I reminded myself. *We are made of stronger stuff than this.* I found a spot where the crowd could see me as we departed. I had to be strong for just a little longer. They would not want to witness their princess departing in tears. Nor would my father be pleased to hear such a thing. It was hardly the display of strength and dignity he expected from me. I waved and the crowd roared.

Tiamat came to stand beside me.

"May Marduk give you strength, Princess," she said.

I cast her a glance, surprised at her thoughtfulness. She stared out at the crowd, although the distance in her eyes suggested she saw nothing of what lay in front of us

"Are you sad to be leaving?" I asked.

"Perhaps not as sad as you. Although I have nothing to keep me here, Babylon is all I have ever known. I never expected to leave and I certainly never expected to travel all the way across the seas to live in a foreign country. However, it is as it is, and I am determined to make the best of it."

"We are not so different, you and I."

Tiamat gave me an appraising look. I was impressed she waited for me to explain rather than rushing to protest that a servant and a princess could never be alike. She was cautious with her words, it seemed, although I suspected she wouldn't hesitate to give her opinion once she had decided it.

"Neither of us chose this fate," I said. "Neither of us desired this for ourselves, but our king has determined that this is what he wants from us. We obey because we must, but we will make a new life for ourselves because we choose to."

"A new life?"

"We have two choices, Tiamat. We can weep and mourn the loss of a country that will forget us as soon as we are out of sight. Or we can decide this will be an adventure and an opportunity to reshape ourselves as we wish."

"You might," she said. "But not me. I am merely a servant. I go where my mistress goes. I do as she says. I have even less control over my life than you do."

"What if I offered to release you from my service and ensured you had funds sufficient to start a new life?"

She looked straight out over the crowd and didn't even glance at me.

"How might that occur?" she asked.

"Attend me until I bear Pharaoh a son and then you may leave if you wish. Serve me well and you will always have a place with me, but if you desire to be released, I will grant it. Until then, though, I expect total loyalty. I travel to a foreign court where I have no allies and no friends. I know nobody there, not even the man who is to be my husband. I need people I can trust. People who will tell me what is whispered about me, what lies or gossip are spread. People who will warn me if I make the wrong move."

She finally looked at me, a long assessing stare as if she measured whether I spoke the truth.

"You can trust me," I said. "But can I trust you?"

Tiamat bowed her head, then touched her fingers to her lips.

"You have my word, Princess," she said. "I will serve you until you bear a son. I will be your eyes and ears at court. But once your son is born, I will expect you to remember your promise."

I touched my fingers to my lips, an unheard-of sign of respect to someone who was of lesser status, but it would signal to her how seriously I took our vow.

CHAPTER 6

$\mathcal{A}$lthough the captain had said he was almost ready to depart, it seemed to take a very long time before the crew hauled up the bridge. A southerly breeze filled the sails and the ship creaked as we set off. I smiled and waved until the crowd was out of sight. The wind surely left my hair in even more disarray than our previous transport, but nobody commented. Tiamat was the only maid who stood at my side as we sailed away. The others had probably found themselves a place to sob and wail. Fortunately, I didn't have to listen to them doing it.

By the time the last of the folk who had come to witness my departure were out of sight, my cheeks were sore and my face felt like it was stuck in a bright smile. At least we were far enough away that they wouldn't see the tears slipping from my eyes despite my determination not to cry. They dried quickly in the breeze, and if Tiamat noticed, she wisely said nothing.

"Well then," she said after I had composed myself. "Do you wish to inspect the boat? Or perhaps you would like to sit and have some refreshments?"

"Have you seen Tall and Half?"

"The…" Her voice quickly died, likely realising it mightn't be wise to call them the idiot and the halfwit, or whatever it was she had meant to say. "No, I haven't. Would you like me to find them?"

I swallowed another sob and nodded. She was gone only a short while before she returned with both men following her.

"Princess!" Tall waved as he spotted me.

Half, always the more reserved of the two, only bowed his head and touched his fingers to his lips.

"Sail!" Tall said.

"Yes, we sail to Egypt," I said. "Do you know where that is?"

"Far!"

"Very far."

"Long!"

"I don't know how long it will take." Nobody had thought to tell me and since most folk thought Tall didn't have enough wits about him to understand anything, of course they wouldn't have told him either.

"I expect it will take a month or so, Princess," Half said. "Assuming fine weather and no pirates."

"Pirates!" Tall's hands flapped and his face showed clear dismay.

"I should have asked if you wanted to come," I said. "But I had to give names and there was no time to send for you. Would you rather have stayed?"

"Boat!" His tone was cheerful and it eased my conscience to know he was happy enough to come with me.

"And you, Half?" I asked.

"Princess, I am sure you are well aware of my status, or lack thereof, in your father's court. One such as myself is limited in employment opportunities, not because of any deficit in my mind, but because folk see only half a man when they look at me. Therefore, if you will have me in your employ, I shall gladly sail the high seas with you."

"Very good." It didn't seem like an adequate response to such an eloquent speech, but I couldn't think of what else to say.

Behind Tall and Half, an old woman approached. She was withered and stooped, and couldn't have been a day younger than fifty. With skin darker than mine, she was clearly not of Babylonian birth. She bowed low and touched her fingers to her lips. Her black hair, which she wore in little braids that fell all the way to her elbows, swung forward as she bowed.

"Are you my new tutor?" I asked.

"Princess, I was told you required someone to teach you the language of my people." She grimaced and rested one hand on her lower back as she straightened from her bow. "I thank you for the opportunity to return to my homeland. I never thought to see it again."

"How long has it been since you left?"

"Oh, thirty years maybe," she said. "Or more. Long enough that I have lost count."

"How did you come to be in Babylon?"

"My husband died." Her voice was emotionless and I assumed it had happened a long time ago. "A work accident that resulted in the loss of his arm. The wound turned bad and he couldn't be saved. It was a terrible death. Very painful. He had debts which needed to be paid, but I had no income and no way of doing such a thing. Everything my husband owned was divided amongst his creditors, including me."

"You were sold to pay off his debts?"

"Not sold, no. Given as payment. My new owner was a businessman. A merchant. He came to Babylon to secure goods for his business and he brought me with him. He did not leave Babylon again."

"He decided to settle here?"

"No, Princess. He died."

The satisfaction in her tone suggested his death had been no accident.

"I have been here ever since," she continued. "Eking out an existence by doing such work as a woman can."

"But do you still remember the Egyptian language? I specifically asked for someone who could teach it to me."

She bowed again and spoke. I knew enough Egyptian to recognise the language, but her speech was rapid and I was dismayed to find I could make out no more than a word or two.

"And can you talk to me of Egyptian culture and customs?" I asked. "I want to know everything about the people before we arrive."

"Of course, Princess. I spent the first twenty years of my life there. Just because one is removed from the country of their birth doesn't mean one forgets everything they knew."

Before I could reply, she hurried on.

"And there are other things I can teach you. More secret things."

"What kind of things?" Always eager for knowledge, my interest was piqued.

She cast a glance towards Tall and Half, and her face became shuttered.

"Things I cannot discuss in public," she said. "Or in front of men."

"Very well then. You will teach me while we sail. Once we reach Egypt, I will decide whether I have further need for you."

"I assure you, Princess, you will need me. You will find I am an invaluable person to keep near to you."

"Valuable!" Tall interjected.

Half hushed him. "Invaluable, she said. It's not the same thing."

Tall gave him a hurt look.

"I think you misunderstood, Half," I said. "Tall meant he, too, would be valuable to me. He wasn't commenting on whether she was or wasn't invaluable."

It was only as I spoke that I realised I didn't know the old woman's name. She had obviously realised as well.

"I am Ahmose," she said. "And I will be a loyal servant if you give me reason to be."

So she saw our relationship, whatever it might be, as a transaction. Was that because of her Egyptian heritage, or was it just how she thought? Either way, I suspected I could learn a lot from the old woman.

CHAPTER 7

We spent the remainder of the day settling into the ship. An area below deck had been prepared for me with soft cushions and blankets, and woollen rugs on the floor. A sturdy wooden bed was bolted to the deck and a curtain enclosed the area to give me some measure of privacy. It was comfortable enough and probably more than I had expected.

Lamps fixed to the walls illuminated the area below deck and wooden chests stacked along the length contained the wardrobe prepared for Ishtar. Nammu and Belit-ili inspected the contents of a couple of the chests, withdrawing magnificent tunics and holding them up to show me, although not without much whispering between themselves. The fabrics were very fine and the embroidery elaborate. Like the tunic I wore today, they wouldn't fit quite right, but there was a queen's wardrobe stored in these chests. I would at least be suitably attired on my arrival and it would be easy enough to have sewers adjust them for me after that.

There were also whole chests of jewels. Finger rings, necklaces and diadems. Bracelets, anklets and belly chains. Pins and beads and bells for my hair. Every kind of adornment I could think of. Father had spared no expense in ensuring his daughter possessed a suitable wardrobe with which to begin her marriage. Within the sole chest containing my personal items were the few jewels I had packed. I felt almost foolish at having brought them. They were nothing compared to the riches prepared for Ishtar.

My first lesson with Ahmose took place the next day. She and I sat facing each other on a rug and as she was about to begin, I noticed Tiamat seemed to have positioned herself where she could listen.

"Did you want to learn too?" I asked her.

"Knowledge about the people we are to live with would be valuable for all of us," she said, casting a glance towards where Tall and Half sat with their backs against the wall. The other maids were nowhere to be seen.

"Of course." I should have thought of that myself. "Find Nammu and Belet-ili."

I called Tall and Half over and explained they would join my lessons. I wondered whether Ahmose would object, but she merely studied them, a thoughtful look on her face. So perhaps the old woman was less judgemental than the folk in my father's palace.

"Learn!" Tall's hands flapped.

"You don't want to learn?" It was rare that I couldn't immediately make sense of his words.

"Idiot!"

"I know that's what people say, but I'm sure you can learn just as well as anyone else. Have you never had any schooling?"

"School!"

His tone had turned sad and he hung his head. I supposed that meant he hadn't.

"What about you, Half?" I asked.

"I did receive some schooling as a boy," Half said. "But that was at least ten years ago. However, I enjoy learning and I would be most pleased to participate."

Ten years? From Half's face, I had thought he was no more than a year or two older than me, but he must be in his mid-twenties at least. Come to think of it, he had looked the same age for as long as I could remember. Had he really not shown any signs of ageing, or had I not paid enough attention?

"Sit down then," I said. "Both of you."

They came to sit on the rug, one on each side of me, so the three of us faced Ahmose.

Tiamat returned with Nammu and Belet-ili trailing her and wearing matching scowls. I gave Tiamat a questioning look and she rolled her eyes. So it seemed the other women were reluctant to participate. I would have thought anyone who was to spend the rest of their life in a foreign country would at least want to be able to communicate with the people there.

"Sit down everyone." My tone was brisk and not inviting of any disagreement. "We have waited long enough. We will meet here every morning immediately after breakfast so Ahmose can teach us Egyptian language and customs."

By the time I finished speaking, Tiamat was already sitting between Half and Ahmose. She and Half gave each other an appraising glance as if each took the measure of the other. Nammu and Belet-ili hung back and neither seemed inclined to join us on the rug.

"Hurry up," I said to them. "Sit down so we can begin."

They exchanged a look and I was sure Belet-ili restrained a sigh. Just as I thought they were going to argue with me, Nammu stepped forward and sat on the other side of Ahmose. To my relief, Belet-ili followed. The only space left by then was between Tall and Nammu. Belet-ili sat unnecessarily close to Nammu, leaving a gap between herself and Tall. He shrank away, moving closer to me as if he sensed her reluctance to be near him. I gave Belet-ili a disapproving look, but she was staring down at the rug and didn't see.

"Well then," Ahmose said. "Let us begin. What do you know of how the world was created?"

"In the beginning, there was water and chaos," I said. Every Babylonian child knew this story. "Then the waters separated into Apsu and Tiamat."

My gaze went to Tiamat before I realised what I did. How did she feel about the name Ishtar had given her? Did she prefer the name her father chose?

"Aah, yes," Ahmose said. "The god, Apsu, of the sweet water, and his goddess, Tiamat, of the salty water."

"And of Apsu and Tiamat were born Lahmu and Lahamu," Half said. "Then Ansar and Kisar."

Ahmose inclined her head towards him and I was pleased to see she didn't seem disposed to treat him like a fool.

"That is indeed as the Babylonians tell it," she said. "We Egyptians tell a different tale. In the beginning, the world was nothing but infinite darkness and waters. Out of this nothingness, Atum willed himself into existence. He created himself in the form of a *bennu* bird and he flew to Iunu. There, as the first rays of the first dawn stretched across the sky, he landed on the *benben*."

Her speech was interspersed with words I didn't know, presumably in the Egyptian language.

"What is a *benben*?" The word was awkward on my tongue as Egyptian always was. Hopefully these lessons would give me not just familiarity, but also confidence with the language.

"A stone pillar," Ahmose said. "Symbolic of the sun's rays. Amun built himself a nest on top of the *benben* before he was consumed by fire and burned to ashes. However, because he was a god and possessed infinite power, he resurrected himself."

"An interesting myth, to be sure," Half said.

"A myth?" Ahmose countered. "What makes it any more of a myth than the tale the Babylonians tell? Who is to say that one people's tale is any more true or correct than another?"

"Same!" Tall said.

Ahmose regarded him seriously and seemed to ponder his statement for a moment.

"There is indeed a sameness to both tales," she said. "In both, a god creates himself out of nothingness."

"Why is it always a god?" I asked. "Why not a goddess?"

"Why indeed?" she shot back at me. "Perhaps it is because these tales are mostly told by men. If we women told our own tales, we could tell them in the way we wanted. We could tell of a goddess who created herself in the beginning."

"Would it still be the truth, though?" Tiamat's voice was tentative and she glanced at me as if she wasn't sure she was permitted to question Ahmose.

The old woman shrugged and didn't seem bothered.

"Who is to say?" she replied. "How do we know what is truth anyway? Who told these tales for the first time? Where did their information come from?"

A tiny shiver passed through my body at Ahmose's words. It was blasphemy to suggest the tale the priests told might not be true, but then, surely the Egyptians thought the same. Who were we to say the Babylonian tale was truer than the Egyptian version? I supposed I would learn many things in my new life and this would probably not be the only one that contradicted the truth I had been raised with.

CHAPTER 8

We settled into life onboard the ship with surprising ease. I saw little of Nammu and Belet-ili except for our morning lessons with Ahmose. That suited me well enough as I had little need of maids on the ship. Once we reached Egypt, I would be stricter with them, but for now I resolved to leave them be. Like all of us, they surely needed time to come to terms with their new lives.

I tried not to think about my parents and Ishtar. I didn't miss my brothers. I had never seen much of them anyway as they were well occupied with their military lessons. Father had not yet decided which son would inherit the throne and he kept them busy proving themselves.

My feelings towards Ishtar were mixed. On one hand, she was my sister and the most dearly loved of my siblings. She had been my only confidante and I couldn't help feeling resentful at her betrayal. She made it impossible for Father to send her to marry Pharaoh and she did it knowing how it would impact on me. I disliked the way we had parted, but I had been too angry to give her a kinder farewell.

I would write to her once we reached Egypt. I would tell her about my marriage to Pharaoh and about where we lived and what my days were like. I might not be able to forgive her yet, but surely I would once I was absorbed in my new life. Once I was queen, it would be easier to forgive Ishtar's betrayal. To forget it was she who was supposed to sit on the throne beside Pharaoh.

I forgot all about Ishtar and my impending marriage as the Purattu emptied into the rougher waters of the Mediterranean Sea. I had never sailed on the open sea before and my stomach rebelled most horrendously. We had barely sat down for our morning lesson when I had to rush up to the top deck and vomit over the side of the boat.

"Princess, are you unwell?" Tiamat asked.

I hadn't noticed her following me. I could only groan in reply as I clung to the boat. My legs trembled and my stomach rolled ferociously. I stared down into the churning waters and promptly vomited again.

"Look up at the horizon," Tiamat said. "Some people do not sail well. It will pass."

"How long?" I asked.

"A day or two."

I groaned as I vomited again. I wouldn't last a day or two. I didn't want to last that long if I would feel like this the whole time. I should throw myself over the side. Let my body sink down into the cold waters and the bliss of oblivion. Then Tall came to stand beside me and he, too, vomited into the sea. Belet-ili and Nammu were not far behind him.

The four of us passed a wretched day, clinging to the side of the boat in our misery. Sinking down to sit on the deck when our legs trembled too much to hold us up. The breeze as we sailed was the only thing that gave me any relief, wicking the sweat from my forehead and the tears from my cheeks. Ahmose came to stand with us for a while and although she looked rather pale, she didn't vomit.

Of all of us, only Tiamat and Half seemed unaffected. They

brought us water to drink and cloths to wipe our faces. Tiamat brought bread, urging us to eat while it was still fresh. There would be no more fresh bread until we reached Egypt. I took a piece, but the mere smell of it was enough to make me vomit again and I tossed the bread into the water.

The crew shot us bemused looks from time to time, as if puzzled by how anyone could be so sick from merely sitting on a ship, but they were too busy to pay us much attention and I was too ill to care when they did.

While the rest of us were occupied with being so unwell, Tiamat and Half spent a lot of time talking quietly between themselves, and at one point I heard her laugh loudly at something he said. It was a laugh of merriment, though, not the usual derisive laugh folk often gave him. I wondered what he had said to make her laugh like that.

When he wasn't with Tiamat, Half stuck close by Tall, reassuring the other man and rubbing his back when he vomited. Tall flapped his hands and seemed more distressed than anyone else at feeling so ill. I saw Tiamat give Half more than one approving look for his kindness towards Tall.

By the time the sun set, Tall had disappeared from the upper deck and Tiamat said he was lying on his blanket down below. He was well enough, she assured me, and Half was sitting with him. By now, my legs were too weak to hold me any longer. My belly still churned fiercely, but there was nothing left in it to vomit. I had passed the last hour sitting on the deck when Tiamat convinced me to go to my bed. She held my arm to steady me and helped me change into a clean tunic.

"Throw that overboard." I nodded towards my vomit-splattered tunic. "The stench will never come out of it."

"It can be cleaned, Princess," Tiamat said. "There is no need to waste a perfectly good tunic."

"As you wish."

I burrowed into my bed with a groan.

"There is a bucket right here beside you," Tiamat said. "And I will bring my blanket closer in case you need me overnight. I will be just on the other side of your curtain."

She unpinned the curtain, letting it drop down to surround my private place. Although it shielded me from view of the others, it didn't block out their noise. Tall and Half talked quietly, or rather Half seemed to be the one doing all the talking, although I couldn't make out his words. Nammu and Belet-ili must have followed us down below because I could hear both of them groaning and sighing. They seemed to make much more noise than was necessary. I heard nothing of Tiamat or Ahmose, and I was still awake when someone blew out the lamps. It was not until much later that I finally fell asleep.

By morning, the nausea had passed. I felt weak and wobbly, but at least I was no longer ill. Tall was already up and looking reasonably cheerful. Nammu and Belet-ili were both awake, but neither seemed inclined to rise. In fact, they groaned and moaned so much I hoped they would stay in their beds.

Tiamat insisted I eat, so I forced down a few bites of bread, although it was already rather stale. After breakfast, we gathered in our usual spot for our lesson with Ahmose, all except for Nammu and Belet-ili. It was preferable to leave them to groan in their beds than to suffer them doing it all through our lesson.

Ahmose began each day's lesson with a new tale from her repertoire of Egyptian stories. Today she told us about how the goddess Isis married her brother, the god Osiris. There was much rivalry between Osiris and their other brother, Seth, who was also a god. Seth murdered Osiris and chopped his body into pieces, which he hid throughout the length of Egypt. Isis searched the entire country until she found all her husband's parts, then she used her magic to put him back together and conceive a child with him.

Ahmose seemed to imply anyone who knew the right magic could do such a thing and I wondered whether this was part of the secret things she had said she could teach me. Given I needed to provide Pharaoh with at least one son, and preferably many, her knowledge could be valuable indeed.

I found Ahmose's tales about the gods confusing. They seemed convoluted and much more complicated than our own stories. But I did my best to make sense of them because this was what the people I would rule over believed. This was what their children were brought up to know. As their queen, it was important I understood their gods and goddesses. I supposed I might even need to worship them myself. After all, would Pharaoh suffer his wife worshipping a foreign god? Would I be permitted to choose which of Egypt's gods or goddesses I worshipped, or would he choose for me? I took Ahmose aside to ask privately, not wanting to share my worry with everyone else, but she only shrugged at me.

"I cannot know, Princess," she said. "The ways of Pharaoh are beyond one such as me. He is a god and is not subject to the laws of man."

That was something else which confused me. Pharaoh was born of a mortal woman, yet he was a god, but not until he was crowned. Pharaoh's sons were ordinary human men, but once one of them took the throne, he too became a god. And when Pharaoh died, he became a star in the night sky, rather than going to the Field of Reeds, which was, apparently, where all other Egyptians desired to go after their death.

Ahmose taught us five new words every day and once we had learnt a word, she insisted we use it rather than the Babylonian equivalent. Already her language felt less unwieldy on my tongue and it gave me hope I would be able to converse without too much difficulty by the time we arrived in Egypt.

Of the others, Tall was the one who struggled the most with

our new language. I often saw him mouthing the words Ahmose taught us, but he seemed unable to say them out loud. I prayed to Marduk he would find a way to speak and that I hadn't brought him to a land where he could communicate with nobody but those from the country of his birth.

CHAPTER 9

*A*hmose's lessons occupied our mornings, but in the afternoons, I often stood on the upper deck to watch our progress through the vastness of the Mediterranean Sea. I was rarely alone at such times with Tiamat usually accompanying me. We practised using the words Ahmose had taught us and I learnt a lot about this woman who had been my sister's maid.

I was surprised to find I quite liked her. She had a calm demeanour and a droll wit which appealed to me. If I could be more like Tiamat, I would easily fit in at my new husband's court. She never seemed to feel awkward, no matter how unfamiliar the situation, or if she did, she hid it far better than I did.

"What is your real name?" I asked her one day.

"It doesn't matter," she said. "Tiamat is the name I have been given and it serves me as well as anything else."

"You can use your real name if you wish."

She gave me a startled look and I shrugged.

"It was Ishtar's rule that her maids take new names," I said. "I don't care what name you use, as long as I know what to call you."

She looked away, out at the ocean for a long time, and I thought she wasn't going to answer.

"Ettu," she said at last in a very quiet voice. "That is the name my father gave me."

"Ettu," I said. "Should I call you that from now on?"

She shot me a look, as if wondering whether I made fun of her. I gave her an encouraging smile and she nodded.

"Yes," she said. "I will be called Ettu."

Half and Tall often came to stand with us as well. Half joined in with our practicing of Egyptian, but Tall was still unable to speak a word in that language, although his comprehension seemed better than anyone else's.

The two men had struck up a firm friendship. Of course, they would have known each other at my father's palace — I myself had known them both for as long as I could remember — but I had never seen them together there. Maybe in a place the size of Dur-Kurigalzu, it was easier for them to keep to themselves. Here, we were forced into proximity with each other. I supposed as two people who were considered outsiders, they had much in common. It pleased me to know they would each have a friend in our new home.

I overheard the odd cruel comment from the crew and it was clear Tall and Half's nicknames had followed them. I chastised a sailor when he said such a thing right in front of me and after that, the crew seemed to keep their opinions about Tall and Half to themselves, or at least they did in my presence. I hoped Pharaoh's palace would be a less judgemental home for such as them. The matter was obviously on Half's mind, too, for he asked Ahmose about it one day.

"Teacher," he said. "Do they have people who look like me in Egypt?"

"I think so," Ahmose said. "I heard about a dwarf once. A woman, if I recall correctly."

She stopped abruptly as if she remembered something she didn't want to say.

"Tell me," Half said. "What happened to her?"

"I think I recall that folk would hire her to perform at banquets."

"Perform?"

"Tell jokes. Sing. That kind of thing. I never saw it myself, mind, and maybe it was somebody else I'm thinking of."

Half fell silent after that and didn't press her for more detail. I wondered if he, like me, doubted that Ahmose's memory was at all unreliable. She seemed to store an incredible amount of information in her brain, and I'd never before heard her sound doubtful about what she remembered.

I saw little of Nammu and Belet-ili outside our lessons. They never once came to practice with us in the afternoons and at meal times they collected their food and then disappeared again. They had laid out their beds in a far corner of the lower deck and hung a blanket to shield themselves from our view. I assumed they were still sulking about being removed from Ishtar's service and I let them be. If they didn't display improved attitudes by the time we arrived, I would dismiss them, but I had no real use for them while we sailed.

We had been at sea for more than a week before I noticed the lack of guards on our ship. I had expected Father would send men to protect me, from pirates as we sailed at least, even if the guards returned to Babylon afterwards. But if any guards accompanied us, they were all on the ships with the gifts for Pharaoh. It gave me an odd feeling in the pit of my stomach to know Father thought I had less need of protection than the riches we travelled with, and I didn't let myself dwell on it.

Busy as I was with my lessons and practicing with Ettu, Tall and Half, our journey passed quickly and almost before I expected it, we heard land had been sighted.

"Princess, they say we should reach Egypt tomorrow morning." Ettu was breathless in her haste to find me.

"Oh." I stared out at the expanse of sea surrounding us. There was still nothing but water in any direction as far as I could see, deep and dark and unforgiving. My mind was suddenly blank.

"Princess? I thought you would be pleased. Are you not looking forward to meeting your husband?"

Show Pharaoh what the women of Babylon are made of. Mother's words echoed through my mind even as a tear slipped down my cheek. I hastily wiped it away and blinked hard before any others could fall.

"Of course I am," I said.

Our voyage had been nothing more than a reprieve. A brief lull before I took up the mantle of wife and queen. Yet these weeks at sea had been some of the happiest of my life. I had unlimited time for learning — always my favourite thing — without feeling like everything I did was constantly being scrutinised. Ettu and I had formed a hesitant friendship. Or at least I thought we had. Her next words made me realise she was never anything but painfully aware of the discrepancy between our statuses.

"I expect you will have a whole army of personal attendants at court," she said. "I trust you will remember our agreement. I will serve you well until you bear a son, but then you will release me and provide me with an income."

"And I expect you to prove your worth to me," I said.

A transaction, like Ahmose expected. I must never forget that both women served me for what I could do for them, not because they cared about me. Loneliness washed over me and I turned my face towards the breeze so it would dry my tears before they fell.

I supposed this was to be my life now. As queen, I would not be in a position to have friends. Folk would pretend to like me, but everyone near to me would have motives. It would be dangerous for me to forget that.

CHAPTER 10

*E*ttu woke me before dawn the next day and I suffered several hours of trying on various tunics in preparation for our arrival to Egypt. She had, it seemed, decided overnight the golden tunic she chose yesterday was unsuitable.

"After all, you are to be queen," she said to me. "You cannot be seen arriving in anything less than what a queen would wear."

Privately, I thought the tunic she chose was perfectly queenly. Made of finely-woven wool died a golden shade, it fell to my knees, below which a gold fringe draped to my ankles. It was one of the finest outfits in the wardrobe assembled for Ishtar.

"Where is the purple tunic?" Ettu asked. "Nammu, check that chest to your left."

Nammu sighed and rummaged through the chest with obvious reluctance. Neither she nor Belet-ili seemed particularly interested in the problem of what I should wear for my grand arrival. I had thought their attitudes would improve if I left them to come to terms with their situation while we sailed, but instead they had grown even sulkier and they muttered constantly between themselves. It seemed their future as maids to the Queen of Egypt didn't please them. Well, I had made no contract with them as I had with Ettu. Hopefully it would occur to them that their continued employment was not guaranteed.

The crew was preparing to dock by the time the women dressed me in the original golden tunic. I restrained my sighs and tried not to look as impatient as I felt. Even once the tunic was on my body, I had to sit still for what seemed like an unbearable amount of time while they made up my face and arranged my hair in an elaborate bun. They adorned me with necklaces, finger rings, bracelets and anklets. Pins studded with semi precious stones dotted my hair.

"I wonder whether Pharaoh himself will be at the docks to greet you?" Ettu asked as she circled me, tugging at my tunic and adjusting the placement of my bracelets.

Belet-ili giggled and quickly covered it with a cough.

"Well, she *is* to be his wife," Nammu said. "I would certainly expect my future husband to be there to greet me if I was arriving from a foreign land."

"I am sure Pharaoh is a very busy man," I said. "I expect I might not meet him until we reach the palace."

"He will at the very least send his highest officials," Belet-ili said. "I wonder if there will be a parade? I would expect a parade if I was to be queen."

"If there was no parade, I'd be starting to wonder whether I was to be queen after all," Nammu said.

"There will be lots of soldiers at any rate," Belet-ili said. "I have heard Egyptian soldiers are particularly handsome and they wear little clothing, day or night."

"Quite fine for those of us who aren't expecting to be queen," Nammu said.

She leaned close to Belet-ili and whispered something that sent the other woman into a fit of giggles. I caught Ettu rolling her eyes. Thank Marduk I had at least one maid with some sense about her.

At Ettu's insistence, we waited down below even once they

were satisfied with my appearance. She worried the breeze from our passage would ruin my hairstyle and leave my tunic in disarray. If I was up above, my maids wouldn't be able to fix me without being seen by the crowd which would be waiting to view my arrival.

"Oh, my." Nammu fanned her face with her hand. "I hope it is not this hot all the time. I fear I am about to faint from the heat."

Belet-ili was quick to agree with her, although Ettu pursed her lips as if it was only a supreme effort that stopped her from responding. Sweat trickled between my shoulder blades, but the temperature wasn't unbearable. It was no worse than Babylon in the peak of summer.

As the ship came to a halt with many creaks and groans, the air down below quickly heated. My hair felt damp and sweat ran down my neck.

"Let's go up," I said. "My makeup will run right off my face if I am down here much longer."

I hurried towards the ladder before anyone could suggest they retouched my face first.

As I emerged from the hatch, I inhaled deeply. My first breath of my new country. I expected Egypt to smell different, that this first breath would be significant. Give me some clue as to what this land was like perhaps. But all I could smell was the salt, the sea, and my own sweat. Ettu was quick to follow me outside and I noticed the deep breath she took as she emerged. She gave me a sheepish grin when she caught me watching.

"I thought it would smell different," she said. "Stupid of me really."

"Me too," I confessed.

"Well, then, are you ready?"

"I'm not sure. But I don't think there's any choice."

We made our way across the deck and I scanned the docks for my greeting party. Guards and officials at the least. Perhaps even Pharaoh himself. Despite what I had said about him being a busy man, I secretly hoped he would be here to welcome his new queen. Surely he longed to see me for the first time as much as I longed to see him.

But there was nobody here other than the dock workers. Men carrying things, guarding things, preparing to transport things. A couple of men who seemed to be giving orders to others. But they were all sailors or soldiers or supervisors. Nobody who looked like they were here to welcome me.

"Where are they?" Ettu asked.

"No parade?" Nammu asked snidely.

"Maybe we have arrived earlier than expected," I said. Yes, that was it. Our journey had been blessed with good weather and we had surely made much better time than anyone anticipated. "I expect the captain will send a messenger to the palace and a greeting party will soon be on its way."

"Perhaps you should wait down below," Ettu said. "So the breeze doesn't mess up your hair."

"It's too hot down there," I said.

Besides, I wanted to see them coming. I wanted the earliest possible glimpse of my new husband. My heart pounded and my legs felt unsteady. Surely I would see him within the hour. I would soon learn whether he was tall or short, fat or thin, old or young. Whether he had a curly beard like my father or a shaved chin.

Most of all, I wanted to hear his voice and know whether he would be a good husband to me. Please Marduk, let Father have chosen a kind man.

CHAPTER 11

The crew carried the chests containing Ishtar's wardrobe from the ship and stacked them on the dock. I waited for more than an hour and still my greeting party hadn't arrived. Nammu and Belet-ili whispered and giggled, although I could hear nothing of whatever it was that so amused them. Would they have whispered about Ishtar like this, or was it only me they had so little respect for?

"I will go check the captain has sent a messenger," Ettu said. She returned quickly, shaking her head. "He says this is as far as he takes us. We will be transferred onto another boat to sail along what they call the Great River. Apparently Pharaoh lives somewhere to the south in a city called Thebes."

I felt rather foolish for not knowing the name of the city to which we travelled. I had assumed the place we arrived in would be my new home, not merely the first stop on our journey. Not wanting to bring Ettu's attention to how naive I was, I kept my thoughts to myself. She must already know I had expected this to be our destination. There was no need for us to discuss it.

"How much further is it?" I asked.

"Another couple of weeks."

A groan escaped me before I could stop it.

"I confess I am rather tired of being on a ship myself," Ettu said.

"Perhaps we will at least have a night on land before we continue." I felt somewhat more cheerful at the thought. "I'm longing for a proper bath."

"I feel like I have salt encrusted all over me. Even my hair is stiff with it."

Another hour passed before the crew began moving the chests again. They loaded them into carts and we were transported to a canal on the other side of the city. Here we would sail to the Great River, which would carry us the rest of the way to Thebes.

"Those boats are rather small," Ettu said as we watched the chests being loaded.

Each boat comprised nothing more than a flat deck with a single mast and sail. The men stacked the chests in what seemed to me to be a rather perilous fashion. I didn't dare ask how the animals would be transported.

"Where are we to sleep?" I asked instead.

"I expect we will stop at towns along the way," Ettu said. "We will surely spend the nights onshore. There really is nowhere for a bed for you."

A wiry little Egyptian man came to usher us onto a boat. He spoke quickly and I was dismayed to discover I couldn't understand as much as I had expected. I made out enough to understand I was to travel on the first boat, which was now ready to depart, but he also used a lot of words I didn't know. He seemed to be saying I could bring only three people.

"I have six attendants who will travel with me," I said to him in halting Egyptian. My three maids, Tall and Half, and Ahmose.

"No, no." He shook his head vigorously. "Three only. No more."

"Princess." Ahmose had appeared at my side. I hadn't seen her or Tall or Half since we disembarked the ship, but I was relieved at her arrival. At least now I could be sure of understanding what the man said. "There is no room for more. You travel with so much luggage that they need the larger boats to transport all your things. You will sail on one of the smaller boats and the rest of your attendants will go with the goods."

"But which three do I choose?" I asked.

Ettu was the most useful of my maids, Ahmose would be valuable for her ability to translate, and I didn't want to separate Tall and Half. It wasn't like Half took up much space anyway. Nammu and Belet-ili could travel separately. I wouldn't miss them at all.

"I will take four with me," I said to the captain.

After all, I was to be his queen. Surely my wishes should count for something. But he shook his head, speaking with such rapidity that I had to look again to Ahmose for a translation.

"Princess, he says this is the last time he will tell you. He says you will do as he says or you can find someone else to transport you to Thebes. He says he does not need the work of transporting argumentative women."

"Argumentative?" My voice came out higher than I expected and I paused to compose myself. "I am hardly being argumentative. There are practical reasons for needing the four I have selected. Besides, doesn't he know who I am?"

Ahmose only shook her head. "His mind is made up, Princess. You can choose three or find another boat."

I sighed. Pharaoh would certainly hear about this lack of respect for his bride.

"Fine then," I said. "Ettu, Ahmose and Tall will accompany me. And I want to speak with Half before we leave."

If I had to separate the two men, Half was the one better equipped to travel on his own.

"I will find him," Ettu said, and hurried away.

I watched as more chests were transferred from the carts to

the boats. I hoped Ettu was correct in thinking we would sleep in towns as I saw nothing resembling beds being loaded onboard.

"Princess."

I jumped when I heard Half's voice at my elbow. Despite his ungainly appearance, the little man moved silently.

"I hear there are some weeks of travel ahead of us yet," he said.

"Half, you will travel with Nammu and Belit-ili," I said. "Tall will come with me."

Regret flashed across Half's face and he bowed.

"For whatever I have done to offend you, I am deeply sorry," he said.

"No, you haven't done anything." I leaned down to him and lowered my voice. "I can only take three attendants with me and I need you to watch those two women. Listen to what they say. I don't know whether we will have the chance to speak again while we travel, but when we arrive in Thebes, I want you to tell me what has occurred between them. Listen particularly for any plans or schemes they make."

"You don't trust them," he said. "Nor should you."

"Do you know something?"

"Nothing specific, but I am a good judge of character. Those two are like vipers."

"So you will watch them for me?"

"I will." He bowed his head and touched his fingers to his lips.

Before I could say anything else, Ahmose called to tell me we were boarding. I nodded at Half and hurried to the boat. Ettu had laid out some cushions for me and I settled myself on them. The swampy aroma of the river filled my nostrils and I breathed through my mouth so I didn't notice it so much. Please Marduk, don't let Thebes stink like this.

Ettu found Tall and told him he was to travel with us. He gave her a cheerful "Sail!" and seemed unfazed at being separated from Half. He found himself a spot next to Ahmose and although they didn't talk, they looked companionable enough.

At the captain's shout, his men pushed the boat away from the dock and rowed out to the centre of the river. As soon as the wind hit the sails, we shot off. The breeze was strong, which seemed fortunate since the current flowed in the opposite direction to which we travelled. I wondered whether the men would have to row if the wind dropped, or if we would merely wait for it to start again. Thankfully, the breeze blew away the river's dank odour and I could breathe more easily.

I leaned back on my elbows and watched the changing landscape. As we left the city behind, the riverbanks became wild and overgrown. Long-legged birds waited in the shallows, perhaps thinking we wouldn't see them if they stood still enough. Ducks and geese sailed with carefree abandon. Insects dipped and dived just above the water's surface and somewhere nearby a frog croaked, then abruptly fell silent. A pair of eyes watched from the water. I couldn't see the rest of whatever beast it belonged to, but it was enough to decide I wouldn't be bathing in the river.

Our passage was much calmer than on the sea, and as I lay back on my cushions, I felt almost content. This country looked very different to my own, but there was a strange, wild kind of beauty to it. Perhaps I could be happy here.

CHAPTER 12

As sunset approached, the crew took down the sail and rowed our boat to the bank. I stood, hoping to catch a glimpse of whatever town we had arrived in, but there was nothing but wilderness for as far as I could see. No people, no buildings, not even a wisp of smoke in the sky to indicate in which direction the town lay. The papyrus and reeds lining the water's edge gave way first to shrubby bushes, then to trees with wide, leafy branches.

"I don't understand," I said to Ahmose. "Where is the town?"

She gave me a confused look.

"Which town, Princess?"

"The one in which we are to sleep. We seem to be in the middle of nowhere."

"We sleep here tonight."

"But where?" I gestured towards the riverbank. "There is nothing here."

"We have the boat." She looked as bewildered as I felt. "We pull in to shore now so we can stretch our legs. We will make fires to cook on. We have everything we need."

"But where am I to sleep?"

"Why, here of course." She pointed to the deck on which we stood.

"We will sleep on the boat?"

"Of course. It is not safe to sleep on the shore, not so close to the river. There are crocodiles and hippopotamuses, and we would provide too easy a meal for them if we were to sleep on the ground."

My head felt light and my face must have revealed my panic, for she quickly continued.

"There is nothing to fear, Princess. We will be perfectly safe on the boat. I'm sure the captain will assign men to keep the fires going all night and to watch over us while we sleep."

Tears threatened and I blinked hard. *Show Pharaoh what the women of Babylon are made of.* I wouldn't shame the Mighty Marduk-apla-iddina by crying over the lack of a soft bed for the night. I didn't even know where the guards Father had sent were, but they were probably too busy watching over the gifts for Pharaoh to guard me while I slept. Ahmose continued, her voice more gentle now.

"I realise it is not what you are used to, Princess, but we will be in Thebes in a couple of weeks."

"Are there no towns along the way? Surely we will not travel from one end of Egypt to the other without passing by towns in which we could stay for the night."

"There are towns, yes, and villages. But they are not always in the place we need them to be when it is time to stop. Our journey would take much longer if we were to lose several hours of light each day for the sake of staying in a town."

"I see."

I didn't really. I'd rather a longer journey if it meant sleeping under a proper roof and in a proper bed and being able to have a proper bath. My arm stung as an insect bit me. I swatted at it and tears welled again. Was this to be my life now?

"We choose how we react to the circumstances in which we

find ourselves," Ahmose said, as if she knew what I was thinking. "We choose to survive or not."

She would know. She had been given to one of her husband's creditors and then taken from her home country, a situation in which she clearly had no control.

"How exactly did the man you were given to die?" I asked.

"I told you there are secret things I can teach you. This is neither the time nor the place, though. Once we reach Thebes and can speak in private behind closed doors, that is when we will discuss such things. For now, I am merely your tutor in the language and customs of my country."

She had killed him, I was sure of it. I couldn't imagine doing such a thing myself. What could possibly make a woman so desperate to escape that she would kill someone?

"Now, see, we are almost at the bank." Ahmose's voice was decidedly cheery. "I don't know about you, but my bladder is fit to bursting."

"Where are we to relieve ourselves? And please don't tell me we simply find a tree."

On the ship, we had chamber pots. I didn't realise at the time how civilised that would later seem.

"Not a tree, no." Ahmose's eyes glinted and she seemed to restrain a grin. "A tree trunk is not wide enough to shield you from view. I would suggest you select a bush. A nice leafy one. You should take off your sandals before you disembark."

She slipped off her shoes, held up her tunic, and accepted the hand of a man who had apparently come to help us down. She landed with a splash and made her way to the shore.

I stared down at the water in dismay. It was thigh-high on Ahmose and I was taller than her, but I hadn't expected to wade through it. Where were the hippopotamuses and crocodiles she had warned me of?

"Is there no bridge?" I asked the man who waited with his hand out to help me.

He gestured towards the bank.

"You see a bridge?" he asked.

His words were rapid, but at least I understood him.

"There was one when we boarded," I said.

"You boarded from a dock. You know, nice wooden boards to make a convenient platform on which to place a bridge? Here, the riverbank is muddy and uneven. There is nowhere to securely set a bridge. If you want to leave the boat tonight, you'll be making your own way to shore."

I gaped at him. Were all the people here so rude? Did they have no respect for their new queen? Before I could find a response, he shrugged.

"I got work to do. Don't have all night to stand here and wait for you to make up your mind."

He walked away, leaving me staring after him.

"Princess!"

Tall had spent the day sleeping and I hadn't spoken to him since we boarded. He peered over the side of the boat.

"Water!"

His voice was cheerful enough that I didn't think he realised we would have to wade to shore. But he jumped down with a splash, shaming me with the reminder that there was nothing wrong with his ability to understand.

"Tall, your tunic," I said.

He looked down at his tunic, which was wet to his knees, and shrugged.

"Dry!"

"Yes, I suppose it will dry eventually."

"Help!"

He held his hand out to me as the rude man had done. I eyed the water again.

"Warm!"

"I wasn't worried it would be cold," I said. "I just didn't want to get wet."

"Help!"

"Yes, I suppose so."

With a sigh, I took his hand, held up my tunic, and jumped down into the water. It was a little deeper than I anticipated and the bottom of my tunic was already soaked through. Tall grasped my hand firmly as we made our way to the shore. My feet sank in the slippery mud and already I had realised my mistake in not taking off my sandals as Ahmose said to.

I desperately prayed the water concealed none of the beasts I spotted earlier, the one who watched us with only its eyes visible above the water's surface. I should have asked Ahmose what manner of creature that was. I would have liked to be able to name the thing I feared as I waded through what might well be its home.

Tall helped me clamber up the bank. More slimy mud. By then, Ettu was right behind us, although I never saw whether someone helped her or if she made her own way. From what I already knew of her, it wouldn't have surprised me to learn she had simply jumped down by herself.

As I tried to wring the water from my tunic, Tall leaned closer.

"Queen!" he said.

"Yes, I know."

"Queen!" His hands flapped.

I patted his arm, unsure what he was concerned about.

"You don't need to worry," I said. "I'll ensure there is a place for you. A job and a bed."

"Queen!" he said, more softly this time.

He sounded sad and I wondered whether I had misunderstood what he was trying to tell me.

Several fires already burned some distance from the shore, a welcoming beacon in a strange environment. Tall, Ettu and I made our way over to one of them. I set my mud-caked sandals beside the fire, hoping they would dry before I had to wear them again, and stood as close as I dared.

"Hot!" Tall took a few steps away from the fire and fanned his face.

"Yes, it is," I said. "But I want my tunic to dry. Yours needs to dry too."

He looked down at himself and shrugged. His wet clothing, it seemed, bothered him less than mine bothered me. I supposed the air was warm enough to dry them overnight anyway. As long as I had dry sandals tomorrow, I could manage the discomfort of a damp tunic for now.

Our flotilla of flat boats lined the riverbank for as far as I could see. I watched for Half, hoping for a chance to ask whether he had overheard anything useful today. Commotion from one of the boats caught my attention. Men shouting. A noise that sounded like an animal screaming.

"What is happening over there?" I asked Ettu.

"They are slaughtering a sheep."

"But those are gifts for Pharaoh."

She shrugged.

"From what I overheard, the captain decided there was no point in men spending their time hunting when we had meat with us."

"But it is not his decision to make," I said. "Nobody even asked me."

Ettu seemed to choose her words carefully before she replied.

"I am not sure they will ask your permission for anything, Princess," she said. "We must remember we are in a foreign land and we don't fully understand the customs of the people here. Perhaps a princess, even one who is to be queen, has no say in the matters of men."

I shut my mouth firmly. I had never seen my father ask my mother's advice on anything, even though she was his queen. So this was no more than I was used to. I couldn't have explained why I had expected to be consulted, other than that I was surely the most highly ranked person in our party. But, so far, I hadn't been treated with even as much respect as had always been shown to my mother. Perhaps the people of Egypt had no regard for their queen.

CHAPTER 13

*E*ttu, Ahmose, Tall and I found a place to sit where the heat of the fire wasn't too fierce, but there was still enough smoke to dissuade the nasty little biting insects. The aroma of roasting sheep soon filled the air and despite my objection at one of the gifts for Pharaoh being slaughtered, my stomach rumbled at the prospect of fresh meat. Our diet on board the ship had mostly comprised salted beef and hard biscuits. The food was plentiful enough to fill our bellies, but monotonous.

We knew the sheep was ready when the men started lining up to receive their portions. I waited, thinking someone would bring my share, but it quickly became clear that only those who lined up would be eating. We joined the queue and soon received sticks threaded with chunks of meat. It was tender and flavoursome, and the juice dripped down my chin as I ate. I felt much more content with a belly full of meat.

The people around us were all men with the exception of Ettu, Ahmose and myself. Nammu and Belet-ili were nowhere in sight. I couldn't see Half either, so I assumed all three were probably together, although I was surprised he didn't seek us out. The men here were taller than those of my homeland and their skin was darker. Their shaved scalps and chins looked too naked to my eye, as did their bodies, clothed as they were in little more than sandals and a knee-length skirt which Ahmose said was called a *shendyt*. It felt indecent to be surrounded by so many bare chests and I kept my gaze on the fire so nobody would think I was staring. Ettu had no such compunctions.

"My, the men here are fine specimens," she murmured to me.

"Ettu." Not knowing how else to react, I pretended to be shocked, but she only shrugged.

"You cannot say it is untrue. They are very different from what we are accustomed to, but I find myself quite liking the look of them."

"There is one over there who has been staring at you all evening," I said with a nod in the man's direction.

She smiled and made a point of looking the other way.

"I noticed," she said.

Soon after we had eaten, folk began making their way back to the boats.

"I suppose it is time for bed then," Ettu said, getting to her feet. "I should find myself a private place first."

"I will come with you."

My bladder was almost ready to burst, but I had felt too shy when we first came to shore to relieve myself behind a bush as Ahmose said. However, nobody would see me in the darkness and it was better to go now than to try to make my way back to shore overnight.

Mud flaked off my sandals and they were far from dry, but I put them on anyway. Marduk only knew what lurked in the ankle-high grasses. Ettu and I found a couple of bushes a short distance away and I averted my gaze as she pulled up her tunic and squatted. I copied her and the relief I felt almost overcame my embarrassment. I would have to do this many times yet with the days of travel still ahead of us.

I remembered to take off my sandals and hold my tunic high before we splashed back to the boats. A man boosted each of us up and I clambered inelegantly onto the deck. Father would be horrified if he could see me, I thought, surprised when a giggle escaped my lips. My tunic hiked up to mid thigh, my feet bare, and my hair likely in disarray from the breeze. But my belly was full and I was not alone. I supposed things were not as dire as they might have been.

Our beds were no more than a blanket spread on the deck. Ettu brought me a cushion for my head, but even so, the hard wooden planks made it difficult to get comfortable. The night air was filled with croaking and chirping and splashing, not to mention the murmurs and coughs and snores of the people around us. With so much noise, it was a long time before I fell asleep.

As dawn broke, the boat's occupants seemed to suddenly come to life. By the time I sat up, hugging my blanket around my shoulders — the air overnight had cooled much more than I expected, considering how warm the day had been — the crew were already preparing to set sail.

"We should go onshore," Ettu said as she folded her blanket. "I am not sure there will be another chance before we stop tonight."

One of the crew helped us down into the water and we hurried to find suitable bushes. By the time we returned, the boats were ready for departure. I set my still-damp sandals aside while my feet dried, feeling stupidly proud of having managed to keep my clothing completely dry this time. Probably not the sort of skill Father had expected me to learn, but it felt like an achievement to me. One small way I was adjusting to my new life.

Breakfast was more of last night's sheep with hard baked biscuits which were suspiciously similar to those we ate on our sea voyage. There were also mugs of beer, much saltier than I was accustomed to and somewhat lumpy. Ahmose had explained last night that beer was drunk through a reed to filter out the largest chunks and I felt rather foolish as I sipped my beer through its straw. I supposed the people here would have many customs that seemed strange to me.

The remaining days of our journey passed in something of a haze. I alternated between dozing and watching the changing landscape. For the first couple of days, we passed through a verdant land where a series of canals led from the sea down to the Great River. Once we reached the river, the landscape became drier. Ahmose explained the country received very little rainfall and relied almost entirely on the Great River's annual flood.

Akhet the people here called it, the season of inundation, when the waters broke the riverbanks and spread over the land. When the flooding retreated a few months later — they called it *peret*, the emergence — it left behind a rich, black soil and it was in this they planted their crops. In *shemu*, they harvested, and then the waters of *akhet* came again. Inundation, emergence, harvest. A continuous cycle of life and re-birth.

It was strange to learn my new country had no rainy season like Babylon. In the rare year when the Great River didn't flood, it meant there was no renewal of the land for the planting of crops. Without the annual flooding, the land was dry and arid, and the people would starve. It was Pharaoh's holy task to ensure the flooding occurred when it should and to the correct height, Ahmose explained. I wondered how a mere man could do such a thing, but she reminded me Pharaoh was a living god. And yet he would also be my husband and would expect me to bear him sons. My mind shied away from the thought of creating a son with a god.

We passed by some kind of settlement every day or two. Sometimes it was a small village comprising no more than a few houses. Others were cities which didn't look all that different from Babylon. One such place was called Memphis and Ahmose told us that Pharaoh sometimes lived here. Not the Pharaoh I was to marry, but others who had come before him. They were now stars in the night sky and only the one Pharaoh remained to be a living god.

One night about a week into our journey, Half found us as we sat near a fire waiting for our meal, which smelled like it would be yet another of the sheep intended for Pharaoh.

"Half!" Ettu gave him a welcoming smile and moved over to make room for him between herself and Tall. He sat down and Tall slapped him on the back.

"See!" he said.

"Yes, buddy," Half said. "It's good to see you too."

"How has your journey been?" I asked. "Have you learned anything?"

"All sorts of gossip and speculation," he said. "Nothing that needs repeating. So far, I've not heard an original thought from either of them."

"Nasty!" Tall said with a frown.

Half nodded. "Yes, most of what they say is nasty."

"I'm sorry you have to put up with them," I said. "I tried to bring you on our boat, but I was told there wasn't room for a fourth person."

"Don't worry about me, Princess," he said. "I am perfectly fine and it's only another few days."

"Me!"

Half sighed. "They talk about everyone, buddy. I'd advise not worrying what those vipers say about you."

"At least you can spend some time away from them tonight," Ettu said. "It's a pleasure to have you with us."

It was hard to tell in the flickering firelight, but I would have sworn Half blushed. He looked away and mumbled something I didn't hear. Ettu replied, her voice also low as she reached over to briefly touch his hand.

We passed the ruins of Akhetaten, where the crumbling

remains of a palace stood not far from the river. Ahmose hissed when she saw it and refused to speak of why the city had been abandoned. Something truly terrible must have occurred here.

When we finally reached Pharaoh's city of Thebes, Ettu dressed me again in the golden tunic and pinned my hair up in a high bun. She applied rouge to my cheeks and coloured powder to my lips, and adorned me with jewellery.

"You look very lovely," she said, stepping back to admire her work. "Pharaoh will surely be enchanted."

"I will make Father proud." I spoke more to remind myself than for her, but she nodded.

"You must," she said. "There is no other choice. Not for a woman such as you whose life is determined by others."

"Is your life not also determined by others?"

She was, after all, in my service. She had no choice but to go wherever I did and that had brought her to this foreign country.

"Yes, but we have an understanding," she said. "Once you have borne Pharaoh a son, I will be free to leave. Then I will determine my own fate. Perhaps it will be here in Egypt. Perhaps it will not."

"You would not want to marry?" I had wondered what her feelings were towards Half.

"And then I would once again be subject to someone else's decisions," she said. "I think I want to find out what my life can be without that first."

I shrugged and didn't reply. It must be nice to have the luxury of determining your own life, but that would never be available to me. *Show Pharaoh what the women of Babylon are made of.* I straightened my shoulders at the memory of Mother's instruction.

I would indeed show Pharaoh. I would make the best of this life Father had chosen for me, but even after I was Queen of Egypt, I would never forget that I, Kassaya, was first a Princess of Babylon.

CHAPTER 14

My arrival into Thebes would be heralded by a greeting party. I knew this for a certainty. The only reason there was nobody to greet me when we first reached Egypt was because we were not expected there. However, I was surely expected here in Pharaoh's own city and he would send a suitable party as soon as he received word of our arrival. Perhaps he would even come himself. I tried not to hope for such a thing, but I longed to know what my new husband looked like.

Having spent days surrounded by half-naked Egyptian men, I had built an image of him. Strong shoulders, a muscled chest. Shaved chin and scalp. Would he dress like the men around me who wore only a *shendyt* and sandals? I had seen few women as we travelled, only glimpses from a distance as we sailed past their cities, so I didn't yet have much sense of what they wore. I supposed it would be different from what I was used to.

I straightened my golden tunic with its fringes that fluttered around my ankles, although Ettu had already ensured it sat perfectly. Would they think my appearance ridiculous? Or backward? In Babylon, this tunic would be considered the height of fashion — it had been made for Ishtar, after all, and she would wear nothing less — but perhaps fashions were different here.

"Princess, is there a problem?"

I had forgotten Ettu's presence until she spoke. I hesitated, wondering how much to tell her. Would she think me foolish?

"Just wondering whether I am dressed appropriately," I said at last, resolving to keep the rest of my thoughts to myself.

She eyed me up and down.

"Never mind," I said quickly before she could suggest I change. "It was a stupid thought."

Tall arrived before Ettu could reply. He had mostly kept to himself during the days as we sailed, seemingly lost in thought as he flapped his hands near his face in the way he did when he was anxious. Perhaps he worried about how the people here would treat him, or whether he would find his place in our new home. When we went on shore in the evening, he seemed his usual cheerful self, so I didn't ask what he was worrying about. Perhaps I should have, I realised suddenly. Perhaps he was more unhappy about leaving Babylon than he had let on.

"Here!" Tall said.

"Yes, I think we are here," I said. "How have you found the travelling?"

"Long!" He gave me a mournful look.

"It has indeed been a long journey and I am rather weary of travelling myself. It is almost over, though. Tonight we will be in the palace and we will be far more comfortable than on the boat."

"Bed!"

"You don't need to worry. I will make sure you have a bed."

I shot a look in Ettu's direction and she nodded before I could say anything else.

"You will likely be swept away and kept busy on our arrival," she said. "I will ensure suitable accommodations are made for both Tall and Half."

"Ahmose too," I said.

"Of course."

Tall reached out to gently touch my wrist.

"Queen!"

"Yes," I said. "Soon."

He sighed and I sensed his frustration at his inability to convey whatever it was he wanted to tell me.

My stomach filled with nerves as we approached the dock. I could see little of my new home, just a few buildings whose purpose I couldn't make out from here. The dock seemed to be filled with working men and I couldn't immediately spot my greeting party. I supposed they would hang back until we arrived. They would not want to get in the way of the workers, after all.

The boat bumped up against the dock and men moved quickly to secure it with rope.

"Here!" Tall said, more quietly this time. He touched his fingers to his lips and it seemed his words were meant to reassure me he was here with me.

"Thank you," I said.

On my other side, Ettu fussed with her tunic.

"Well, this is it," she said.

My legs trembled and I couldn't reply, suddenly sure I would vomit if I opened my mouth.

As we disembarked, there were men everywhere I looked. With such a number of boats arriving at the same time, there was much work to do in unloading them. And this wasn't even all the contents of the ships we had sailed with. There hadn't been enough boats available when we arrived to transport everything at once. Most of the gifts for Pharaoh would follow behind us.

"Move," a man growled, almost knocking me off my feet as he carried a chest from the boat.

"Perhaps we should wait over there." Ettu pointed to an area that seemed less crowded. "I am sure there will be someone here shortly to greet us."

"I suppose they didn't know exactly when we would arrive," I said. "Someone has probably sent a messenger to the palace to alert them."

I felt much better once I realised this. Of course, they wouldn't have known the exact time to expect us. No messenger had been sent on ahead of us while we sailed as far as I knew. So we would have to wait while the news travelled to the palace, but Pharaoh would surely send a greeting party as soon as he heard. I could still hope he might come himself.

We waited while the boats were unloaded. The sun beat down relentlessly and there seemed to be no shade anywhere. Sweat trickled down my neck and my makeup had surely run right off my face.

"Princess."

Half's arrival was a relief, even if only for the distraction from waiting and wondering how much longer my greeting party would take.

"Half, how was your journey?" I asked.

"Well enough, but I must warn you quickly. There is some plot afoot with those two, although they were circumspect about what they said in front of me. There were many sniggers and pointed comments, though, which made me suspicious."

He stopped and looked around, although at his height he could surely see little more than the legs of the working men.

"Are you waiting for transport?" he asked.

"My greeting party should be here soon. I expect a messenger has been sent to the palace to alert Pharaoh to my arrival."

He nodded, a thoughtful expression on his face.

"How long do you intend to wait?" he asked.

"Why, until they get here," I said. "Are you suggesting there is something else I should do?"

"No, Princess. Only wondering what you intend to do if there is no greeting party."

"But of course there will be. I am to be queen. It has been negotiated between Father and Pharaoh. He expects my arrival."

Nammu and Belet-ili wandered over to stand nearby, albeit just far enough away to make it seem we weren't travelling together, and the rest of whatever Half wanted to tell me went unsaid. They bowed their heads to me, but said nothing, even though we had been apart for days. The smug looks on their faces made me wonder what Half had learned, but I would wait until I could speak to him in private. Nammu gave Half a scornful look and he made a point of turning his back to her. If she still couldn't see his worth, that said more about her character than his.

Although we waited until the last of the boats were unloaded, still nobody arrived to greet me.

"Surely the custom would be to send somebody to fetch the queen," I said to Ahmose.

"I know little about such things," she said. "I never met Pharaoh or any of his family, although I saw one of his sons once."

"Pharaoh already has sons?"

The son I gave him was meant to strengthen the alliance. My son was supposed to inherit the throne. But Ahmose shrugged and didn't look concerned.

"It may not have been the same Pharaoh," she said. "Perhaps it was his father."

Still, worry niggled at me. What if the situation here was not what Father had been led to believe? What if Pharaoh did indeed already have sons? Heirs, even. How would my marriage serve to bond our two countries if he didn't need a son from me?

"No point worrying about it," Ettu said. It was only when she spoke that I realised I was frowning. "We are here now and we will have to make the best of the situation, whatever it turns out to be."

I rearranged my face and tried to appear unconcerned.

"Of course," I said. "I am here to do my duty and marry

Pharaoh. I am sure Father is aware of all the details and everything has already been agreed."

Nammu sniggered, which quickly turned into a cough when I glared at her.

The contract between Father and Pharaoh surely specified my son would be heir. I couldn't see any reason Father would have sent one of his daughters if he didn't expect such a thing. Mother certainly did. She had made a point of telling me my son would be heir. *But Father doesn't tell Mother everything,* a nasty voice inside my head whispered. *She might not know any more than you do.*

I smoothed my tunic and tried to tell myself I wasn't worried. It had all been arranged. Father had done what he thought was best.

The boats were unloaded and restocked with provisions before they set off to make their way back up the Great River. There was no need for sails this time. The crew merely had to row out to the centre of the river where the boats caught the current and shot off.

And still my greeting party hadn't arrived.

CHAPTER 15

"Princess, perhaps we should make our own way to the palace?" Half suggested eventually. "The sun is starting to set and whatever arrangements they are making there are taking far too long. We might wait long into the night before anyone arrives to fetch us."

"I agree," Ettu said. "We may as well go. Perhaps they will meet us on the way."

Nammu whispered to Belet-ili, who tittered behind her upraised hand. I pretended not to notice. It might have been nothing about me and I would only look foolish and paranoid if I asked. I needed to know what Half had learned before I made any move against them.

"What about the gifts for Pharaoh?" I asked. "And my luggage."

Ahmose went to find out and soon returned with news that men had been assigned to watch over the goods until arrangements could be made to send everything to the palace. It likely wouldn't be long. Pharaoh would surely not delay taking possession of the riches sent with me.

Nammu and Belet-ili huffed and groaned when they learned we were to walk.

"So much for arriving with the new queen," I overheard Nammu muttering.

"I expected to be transported in style," Belet-ili murmured back and they both giggled.

I pretended I hadn't heard. Were these the kind of pointed comments Half meant? It seemed odd they apparently saw no reason to be respectful, given their continued employment depended entirely on me.

Ahmose obtained directions to the palace and we set off. A blister developed where my sandal rubbed against my little toe. I gritted my teeth and didn't let myself complain. We would surely encounter the greeting party sooner or later, and they would have transport for me. A palanquin maybe, or a beast to ride. I wouldn't have to walk all the way to the palace.

But walk all the way was exactly what we did. Darkness fell and with it came my first view of the Theban night sky. It loomed over us, dotted with the stars the people here believed were past pharaohs. If that was true, they must have had many thousands of pharaohs.

The palace was an imposing building silhouetted against the night sky. Burning torches lit a pathway to the front doors. Lamplight shone around the edges of the windows, already shuttered against the biting insects that descended as soon as the sun set. I slapped them away from my arms and tried to feel grateful we would soon be indoors.

Guards stood in front of the enormous wooden doors at the entrance to the palace. They each held a spear and their other hand rested on a dagger secured in their belt.

"Halt," one of them said. "State your business."

I hesitated, not having expected to be in the position of introducing myself. I had been so sure they were expecting me. To my immense relief, Half stepped forward.

"Good evening." He spoke slowly, although his mastery of the

Egyptian language was a little better than mine. "I present to you Kassaya, Princess of Babylon."

"And what is her business?" the guard asked.

"She is come to marry Pharaoh, of course," Half said.

"Oh, you want the Palace of the Ornaments." The guard took his hand from his dagger and pointed further up the street. "That way. Another hour or so past here."

"I think you mistake me," Half said smoothly. "Is this not Pharaoh's residence?"

"It is," the guard said. "But the Ornaments don't reside here. They have their own palace."

"Perhaps you could call for Pharaoh," I said. One of the guards sniggered. "Or his representative," I added quickly. "I'm sure we can clear up this confusion if we can just speak to the right person."

"There is no confusion," the other guard said, the one who didn't snigger. "If you are to be an Ornament, you need to go to the Ornaments' palace."

"I don't understand what an Ornament is," I said. "It is not relevant to me. I am here to marry Pharaoh. I am to be his queen."

"Sorry," the guard said. "If you were expected, we would have received word of it. Usually the Ornaments just go straight to their own palace. Pharaoh will send for you when he wishes to see you."

"I don't think we have any other option," Ettu said quietly to me. "We could stand here all night and argue with them, but they don't seem like men who will change their minds."

I sighed and tried to ignore my throbbing toe where my sandal had surely rubbed the skin right off.

"Let's go then," I said. "I would have thought they would at least have the courtesy to offer us refreshments and a chance to sit down."

I spoke loudly enough for the guards to hear, but if they

understood I meant they were being rude, they paid no notice. Neither of them spoke again as we left.

"Walk!" Tall's voice was mournful.

"I know." I tried to make my voice brisk and cheery. "We have further to walk yet. Might as well get on with it. I am longing for a hot bath."

Our pace was somewhat slower this time, but even so, Ahmose struggled to keep up. She never complained, but her shoulders were hunched and her feet scraped against the road. I wished I could tell her to wait until I could send someone back with transport for her, but after the reception I had received so far, I didn't want to offer something I might not be able to arrange. These people seemed to have no respect for the woman who would be their queen.

I puzzled over the guard's comments about Ornaments, trying to distract myself from the increasing pain where my sandals wore at other patches of skin. Tall limped, and both Nammu and Belet-ili dawdled behind us, although at least they no longer whispered to each other. Half rubbed at his lower back from time to time. Only Ettu seemed unbothered, although she was unusually silent.

At least the road was smooth and easy to walk on. It would be an even more difficult journey if we traversed fields. Buildings lined each side of the street, houses probably from their sizes. Lamplight flickered behind the closed shutters, enticing aromas reached my nose, and the laughter and chatter of families enjoying their evening together reminded me of dinners at home with Ishtar and Mother and Father when he was being just Father and not the Great and Mighty Marduk-apla-iddina.

The moon was well on its way up into the sky by the time we approached another building of imposing size. A great wall surrounded it, hiding all but the top floor from our view. Like Pharaoh's palace, it too was lit up with torches and we made our way to the gates where a pair of guards waited. Just like the last ones we encountered, they were armed and alert.

Once again, Half stepped forward and introduced me.

The guards looked me up and down, but it wasn't the cold, disinterested stare of the other guards.

"I am afraid your male companions will need to remain out here," one of them said, and his tone was so respectful that I was taken aback even before I realised what he had said. Tall's hands flapped. He had understood them before I did.

"No, they will come with me," I said.

"Men are not permitted within these walls," the guard replied.

"My companions have travelled with me all the way from Babylon," I said. "And they will all remain with me."

The guards glanced at each other and one of them seemed to shrug a little before they turned back to me.

"Does any of your party carry weapons, my lady?" a guard asked.

"I don't think so," I said. "Do any of you have a weapon?"

Half produced a small dagger from the belt of his tunic.

"I'll have to take that from you," the guard said. "No weapons are permitted in the Palace of the Ornaments."

Half shrugged and handed it over.

"No other weapons?" the guard asked, eyeing Tall.

"Weapon!" Tall said.

"He means no, he doesn't have any," I said.

The guard gave him a puzzled look, but only shook his head. He gestured to the other fellow who began opening the gates.

"Welcome to the Palace of the Ornaments," the guard said. "Follow the path up to the Palace and someone will attend to you there."

He pointed, although it was unnecessary as the path was lit by a series of torches which clearly indicated where we were to walk. The others hesitated, probably expecting me to go first.

For the whole journey from Babylon to Thebes, I had believed I knew what awaited me here. I would marry Pharaoh and be his queen. I would integrate myself with the people who lived here and they would accept me. Perhaps one day they would even love me.

But nothing seemed as I had expected. Nobody came to greet me. I couldn't even get inside Pharaoh's palace, where I had expected to live. And now I was here, in the place they called the Palace of the Ornaments. I had no idea what awaited me, but it seemed that whatever it was, it would be very different from the fate I thought I was sent to. I wished someone else could lead the way down the path.

CHAPTER 16

With only the torches to light our way, I could see little beyond their light. Shadows loomed in the darkness beyond. Tall ones — trees, I presumed. Shorter ones likely bushes or shrubs. Others might be garden beds. Indeed the air was fragrant with perfume, suggesting the gardens contained many flowers in bloom. Already my nose itched and a headache loomed. Tall sneezed.

"Smell!" he said.

"Yes, buddy," Half said. "It is indeed a strong smell."

"Delightful," Ettu said. "I'd rather smell flowers than body odours."

"Oof!"

"I don't think she meant you," Half said.

A shape moved in the darkness and I stopped. Someone bumped me from behind, sending me pitching forward a couple of steps. Tall was swift to grab my arm before I fell on my face.

"See!" he said.

"Yes, I saw it too," I said.

We all edged a little closer together and my heart suddenly pounded. There was something wrong with this situation.

The way nobody seemed to be expecting me.

Being directed away from the palace and to some other place where everything was in darkness and we were sent off to follow a path alone.

What if the alliance was a sham? What if Pharaoh intended to betray Father by doing something to me? My mind baulked and refused to consider the possibility of what *something* might be.

Show Pharaoh what the women of Babylon are made of.

"Who is there?" I called. "Show yourself."

A childhood of being raised in public, always on display to anyone who entered Father's court, held me in good stead and my voice sounded strong and confident.

The shadow moved again. It loomed closer. My heart thudded so hard, I couldn't hear whether the shadow made any noise.

A man stepped into the light. He bore no weapons that I could see, but the way he held himself told me he was trained. A guard perhaps, or a soldier.

"Sorry to have alarmed you." His voice was courteous and he gave a shallow bow. "I patrol the gardens after dark. Keeping an eye on everything."

My legs went weak with relief. For a moment, all I could do was breathe. Fortunately, Ettu responded before the man had time to think we were all simpletons.

"Are we close to the Palace of the Ornaments?" she asked. "We were told to follow the path, but it seems a very long way."

"It's only a little further," he said. "The Palace is just past those trees."

He gestured, but I could see nothing other than darkness and shadows.

"Thank you," I said. "We shall be on our way then."

"I will see you there."

He stepped onto the path and started off in the direction he had indicated.

"I was not expecting any arrivals tonight." His tone was conversational.

He walked ahead of me and I could see nothing of him but his back. Unlike most of the men we had seen here, he wore a linen shirt with his *shendyt* and sandals. I wondered whether the purpose of his shirt was to conceal weapons. Surely if his job was to watch for intruders, he would not do it unarmed, despite what the guard had said about weapons not being permitted. But then, there weren't supposed to be any men in here either.

"It seems we were not expected," I said.

He shot a glance at me over his shoulder.

"Are you the one who is to stay here?" he asked.

"I am. My name is Kassaya and I am the daughter of Marduk-apla-iddina."

"And where does Kassaya, daughter of Marduk-apla-iddina, hail from?"

"Babylon."

"I see." He was silent for a moment, as if digesting this news.

So, I really wasn't expected or he would have made some comment like, *oh, we didn't think you would arrive until next week.*

"And you are?" I asked.

"Khaemmalu, my lady. You won't see much of me, though, unless you have a tendency to wander the gardens at night."

"As it seems I do."

Embarrassment filled me at the words that had come out of my mouth. It sounded like I was flirting with him. My cheeks heated and I hoped nobody would notice in the flickering torch-light. I hadn't intended it like that. I was here to marry Pharaoh. I wouldn't shame either him or my father by flirting with some guard I encountered in the garden.

Khaemmalu didn't respond. Did that mean he hadn't thought I was flirting, or he did and he was being careful not to encourage me? Marduk, what a mess.

We passed through a treed archway, then suddenly the Palace

loomed in front of us. In the darkness it seemed endless, lit up with torches every few paces. Windows dotted its facade, which stretched as far as I could see. They were all shuttered, some with lamplight shining around the edges and others in darkness. A guard stood on either side of the front doors. More men. They appeared to be unarmed, although, like Khaemmalu, they wore shirts.

"There you go then," Khaemmalu said, somewhat unnecessarily. "The Palace of the Ornaments awaits you, my lady."

He bowed, then backed away into the darkness. Before I could thank him for escorting us, he was gone.

My feet were rooted to the path. This felt like a big moment. Bigger even than stepping through the gates of the Palace of the Ornaments. Maybe the biggest moment of my life.

I could walk forward into the destiny Father had sent me to, even if I suspected what awaited me was not what he had chosen.

Or I could retrace the path we had just taken. Go back out through the gates. The guards were surely there to keep people out, not to keep them in. I could leave now. Flee. Find some other future for myself. I couldn't go home — not if I rejected what Father had decided for me. He already had one recalcitrant daughter to deal with. He would be even less tolerant of a second.

Before I could decide, Ettu stepped forward.

"Well, then," she said. "I don't know about anyone else, but I have really had enough of all this walking."

And suddenly the possibilities disappeared. There was no choice. Not for me. Marduk-apla-iddina had sent me to be Pharaoh's bride. I could only move forward.

Show Pharaoh what the women of Babylon are made of.

CHAPTER 17

The door guards watched our approach, seemingly less concerned than the ones at the front gates. It was only when we were right in front of them, that one held up his hand to stop us.

"It is rather late for an arrival tonight," he said.

Like Khaemmalu, his tone was conversational, but I got the feeling he took in everything about us. His gaze darted from person to person. Ettu, who was still in the lead. Me, with Tall and Half close behind. Ahmose, Nammu and Belet-ili brought up the rear, although he probably couldn't see them in the shadows. After inspecting each of us, his gaze came back to me.

"And you are?" he asked.

"Kassaya, Princess of Babylon and daughter of Marduk-apla-iddina. I have been sent to marry Pharaoh to seal the alliance between Babylon and Egypt."

It was possibly the most I had said in Egyptian and my speech sounded awkward, even to my own ears. If the guard was at all impressed, his face didn't show it. He merely knocked on the door behind him and called out.

"Send a messenger to the administrator. A new Ornament has arrived."

"What exactly is an Ornament?" Ettu asked. "We keep hearing that word, but nobody has yet explained what it means."

The guard didn't even look at her.

"All will be explained in due course," he said. "And not by me."

Ettu huffed. I supposed as maid to a princess, she wasn't used to being treated so rudely. I would have liked to chastise the guard, but my status here seemed uncertain, so I kept my mouth shut. Whatever an Ornament was, it didn't seem to be someone who was respected.

We waited.

My feet ached and my legs were tired. I longed to sit — on the path or the grass, I didn't care anymore — except I didn't want to damage the golden tunic, and sitting outside the Palace would surely lower my status even more in the eyes of the people here. Instead, I pulled back my shoulders and raised my chin. The guards didn't need to know how defeated I felt. I was a princess of Babylon and that was what they would see when they looked at me.

After what felt like at least an hour, the doors opened and a man emerged. His shaved head glistened in the torchlight and, like the guard, he studied each of us before his gaze settled on me.

"Welcome," he said. "Please come in. I apologise there was nobody to greet you at the gates, but we were unaware you would be arriving tonight. However, a chamber has been made ready for you and there is a place for your women servants."

Ettu stepped forward, but I didn't follow her. Was he implying Tall and Half couldn't come with me?

"These two men also serve me," I said.

The administrator gave me a tight smile.

"Very few men are permitted inside the Palace of the Ornaments and those who are, are personally approved by Pharaoh himself. I regret I cannot allow your menfolk inside."

"So where are they to go?" I asked. "I assume you have made other accommodations for them?"

He cocked his head to the side and seemed to regard me with something that might have been either puzzlement or amusement.

"They are of no concern to me," he said. "My task is to see to the comfort of the residents. Your men will need to make their own arrangements."

"But we have only just arrived in Thebes. We know nobody and they have nowhere else to go. Surely you could allow them to stay for the night. It is far too late for them to be wandering the streets of a foreign city, looking for somewhere to sleep."

He gave a great sigh, as if I was being unreasonable.

"I suppose they could sleep in the stables," he said. "Just for tonight. They are to be gone by dawn and I do not expect to see them here again."

I didn't bother to reply to him, but turned to Tall and Half.

"We will figure something out in the morning," I said. "As soon as I can meet with Pharaoh, I will raise this with him. Surely he will allow you to stay with me if I insist."

"Don't worry about us, Princess," Half said. "We can look after ourselves."

The administrator returned inside and I heard him speak, although his voice was too low for me to make out his words. A young man of perhaps seventeen or eighteen years emerged.

"Come with me," he said, beckoning to Tall and Half.

I watched them depart, then turned back to the administrator.

"Considering you said there were few men, there seem to be an awful lot of them around here. So far, we have seen nobody other than men."

Something flickered in his eyes. Anger, perhaps.

"The men you see within the palace grounds do not enter the

Palace itself," he said. "Ever. They are here for your protection. Those who are permitted within the Palace have been *modified* to ensure they do not interfere with the residents."

His heavy stress of the word indicated this was of great significance. Not wanting to appear ignorant in front of him, I resolved to wait for a private moment to ask Ahmose what he meant.

The administrator held the doors open wider.

"If you are ready then," he said. "Please, do come in."

I expected Ettu to lead the way, but she stood aside and waited for me to go first.

With my heart pounding, I finally entered the Palace of the Ornaments.

CHAPTER 18

We emerged into an expansive foyer. Torches set within sconces on the walls shed a cheery glow over the place. Painted images of women wearing long, white gowns and strange headdresses — goddesses, perhaps — covered the whitewashed walls. The floor bore a tiled mosaic of fish and birds, and potted plants in the corners made the space inviting. Three doors led in three directions.

"This way please." The administrator gestured towards the door to our left. "Your servants may wait here. Someone will attend to them shortly."

"Where will they be taken?"

"We have suitable accommodations for your women," he said, and his voice was almost kindly now. "Your concern for them is a credit to you, but they will share chambers with other servant women and will be available to you when you want them. They will be sent to you in the morning. For now, though, let me see you to your chamber."

He hustled me through the doorway without any chance to farewell my maids and Ahmose. The door closed behind us with a soft swish and we stood in a long hallway paved with tiles in bright blues and greens.

"Come now," the man said, striding down the hallway.

I wished he would walk more slowly so I could inspect the paintings on the walls. They seemed to be a scene from the banks of the Great River with rushes looming over water so skilfully painted, it almost looked like it was moving. There were spiky papyrus plants, soaring birds, and a fish caught in the act of jumping out of the water.

"Will you tell me your name?" I asked as I hurried after him.

"Oh, do forgive my rudeness. I have been rushing to ensure preparations were made for you and I have entirely forgotten my manners. I am Amankhau, second administrator in charge of the Palace. I ensure things run smoothly and that the Palace is kept in suitable condition for the happiness of its residents."

He spoke swiftly and it felt like it took me a little too long to make sense of everything he said. He kept walking and didn't seem to expect a reply.

"How many people live here?" I asked.

"Several thousand."

Amankhau stopped in front of a door and pushed it open.

"This is your chamber," he said. "I do hope you will find it suitable."

I entered and found myself in an expansive space which was easily double the size of my bedchamber in Father's palace. The bed was neatly made with blankets and several cushions. The tiled floor — more of the blue and green design from the hallway — was covered with soft rugs. Large vases in the corners displayed artful arrangements of reeds and dried flowers. Several cushions positioned by low tables provided a place to relax and chat with guests. A long couch under an expansive shuttered window gave the occupant somewhere to sit and look out over what I presumed would be immaculately manicured gardens.

"Will this be adequate for you?" Amankhau asked. "We can, of course, make any changes you desire. Repaint the walls or retile the floors. Different furniture and what not."

"Yes, yes." I finally found my words. "This looks lovely."

"You may note there are no storage chests. I presume you are travelling with chests of your own. I will have them brought to you when they arrive, or if you prefer new chests, I can have some brought in and your things will be transferred into them for you."

"Thank you. My chests are still at the dock, although we left guards with them."

"Nothing is too much trouble for Pharaoh's Ornaments," he said. "Pharaoh wishes you to be comfortable so anything you desire can be arranged. You only have to tell me what you want."

"What exactly is an Ornament? People keep using that word and I don't understand it."

"Pharaoh's wives, of course."

"His wives?" I must have misunderstood. Surely the word he used didn't mean what I thought it did.

Amankhau gave me a puzzled look. "You were not expecting to be an Ornament?"

"Well, no. I expected to marry Pharaoh, but I wasn't aware I would be one of several wives."

"Oh, no, you mistake me." He gave an awkward chuckle. "Pharaoh doesn't have merely several wives. He has hundreds of Ornaments."

My heart sank. This was not what I thought I came here for. Surely, it was not what Father thought he had agreed to.

"Hundreds?" I asked faintly. "So when you said before that thousands of people live here, did you mean..."

My voice trailed away and I couldn't make myself say it.

"Of course," Amankhau said. "Pharaoh's Ornaments all live here, along with many servants for your comfort. As I said, anything you desire can be arranged for you. Nothing is too expensive or too difficult. Pharaoh grants an unlimited budget for the comfort of his Ornaments. Now, I shall leave you to rest. Do you wish bathing water to be brought to you? Wine or food?"

"No. That will be all."

Tears welled, my mind whirled, and I couldn't think. I knew I was probably being rude, but I suddenly needed to be alone. Amankhau bowed and left, closing the door softly behind him.

Alone in my opulent new chamber, a tear finally escaped and trickled down my cheek. I wiped it and blinked hard before the others could fall. This was my life and Father would expect me to make the best of it. I wouldn't stand here and cry. *Show Pharaoh what the women of Babylon are made of.*

I had no sleeping gown to change into, but it hardly mattered since I was alone in this enormous chamber. I pulled off my jewels and tossed them onto a rug. Let a servant pick them up in the morning since apparently there were so many people here for my convenience. I discarded the golden tunic on the floor and kicked off my sandals. A servant could deal with those too. I pulled back the blankets and climbed into my new bed.

Despite my exhaustion, I couldn't fall asleep. My mind whirled, my feet throbbed, and my chest was so tight, I felt like I couldn't breathe. Eventually, I gave up. With the blanket wrapped around my shoulders, I went to the window. When I unhooked the shutters, they swung open smoothly without even the slightest creak.

The first rays of the dawn sun peeked over the wall surrounding the palace. I had thought the wall was intended to keep people out. Now I wondered whether it was designed to keep Pharaoh's Ornaments in.

Would Father have sent me here even if he knew I would be relegated to a secondary palace to live with all the other women Pharaoh had already claimed as his wives? Was this really the fate he had intended for Ishtar, his most favoured daughter? Surely he would not have sent her with any less expectation than that she would be queen.

But then, he hadn't actually told me I was to be queen, had he? He said only that I would marry Pharaoh and he bid me to give Pharaoh many sons. I never heard him tell Ishtar she would be queen either. I wasn't present when he told her of the arrangements that had been made and all I knew was what she told me afterwards. It was Ishtar who told me she was to be queen. Perhaps she too had assumed, or maybe she knew all along. That might have been why she went to such drastic lengths to avoid coming here. Maybe Father knew exactly what he was sending me to.

You were fortunate, Ishtar, I muttered to myself. *If I had known what waited for me here, I might have gotten myself with child as well.*

I was still standing at the window some time later when a knock came at the door. The sun was several fingers' width above the wall now, although I had seen none of its rising, nor noticed the immaculate gardens it revealed. The knock came again.

"Enter," I called.

The door opened and in came Ettu, Nammu and Belet-ili. Behind them followed another seven women. All of them, even my own maids, dropped to the floor to lie on their bellies.

"What are you doing?" I asked. "Ettu, what is this?"

"This is how servants approach their mistress here, my lady." Ettu's voice was muffled with her face still pressed to the floor.

"My lady?"

"It is how noble women are addressed."

"Get up," I said. "All of you."

They rose smoothly, even Ettu, Nammu and Belet-ili who had surely never done such a thing before in their lives. I guessed someone had tutored them overnight in how to get up and down from their bellies so gracefully. I would have looked much more awkward, even used as I was to kneeling.

"Who are these?" It was only as I nodded towards the other women that I realised I was speaking in Babylonian.

"Your lady's maids, my lady," Ettu said and to my relief she, too, used Babylonian. "I have been assigned as your chief lady's maid, in charge of the nine others who will attend to you."

Nammu muttered something and I ignored her. She wouldn't be happy with Ettu's promotion and I didn't intend to encourage any whining from her.

"I have ten maids?" I asked. "Why in the name of Marduk do I need that many?"

Ettu's face was tight and I guessed she had been advised about more changes than that.

"Apparently Pharaoh desires that his wives live in absolute comfort," she said. "Your lady's maids are to ensure your every want is met. If we cannot fulfil something you wish for, there are other servants we can call on. Everything you want is to be provided and as servants, our presence in the Palace of the Ornaments is tolerated only so long as our lady is satisfied with our performance."

I wondered what I was to do with myself all day if there were so many people who had the express purpose of doing things for me. But Ettu wasn't finished.

"We are to ensure you are never alone," she said. "Pharaoh wishes his wives to have company at all times so they are not lonely."

"What if it is my wish to be alone? Would you not have to accede to that?"

"I am sorry, my lady, but it seems that is the one thing we cannot do." She turned to the other women and spoke to them in Egyptian. "My lady will want her breakfast and we need to dress her. Go find clothes and jewels for her. Her own things have not yet arrived. Send someone to fetch hot water. I am sure she would like to bathe before she leaves her chamber."

The women started moving, chattering as they went. Nammu

and Belit-ili moved more slowly and didn't seem to be included in any of the conversations. Ettu inclined her head slightly towards the window and went to stand in front of it. I followed her and we both looked outside.

"There are other things you should know," she murmured, speaking again in Babylonian. "You are permitted no contact with anyone outside of the Palace. If you seek such contact, we are to report it to Panouk, who is the man in charge. You may send letters, but everything is to go through Pentau, the Palace scribe."

"I cannot even write to my father without someone else reading it first?" I asked.

"You cannot write your own letters. You will dictate them to Pentau and he will write them for you. I don't know if he uses Babylonian cuneiform, but apparently he can write in Akkadian. If your father can't read that himself, he will surely have scribes who can."

"I assume if Pentau doesn't agree with something I want to tell my father, he will simply not write it."

"That would be my assumption too."

"What else have you learned?"

"There are many, many wives. The one named Isis-Tahemd-jere holds the titles of Great Royal Wife and Lady of the Two Lands. She lives with Pharaoh in his main palace."

So that was his queen. The position I had expected to hold myself.

"Here at the Palace of the Ornaments, there is a woman called Tiye," Ettu continued. "She is considered the most highly ranked of all the Ornaments and is second only to Isis, as far as I can tell. When Pharaoh comes to visit, it is she he spends the most time with, and she often attends festivals and special events with him as his wife."

"But she is not a queen?"

"I don't think so. The women here believe that if Isis were to die, Lady Tiye would take her place as Great Royal Wife. I think that means she would also be queen."

What hope was there for me then? Even if something happened to Isis, there was another woman already in line for her position, and potentially several hundred others waiting to take her place. Why am I here, Father?

"How did you learn this?" I asked.

"The servants talk. They know every detail about what happens within the Palace. Who talks to who. Who is plotting against who. Who is sleeping with who. You should be careful what you say in front of the servants. Not just your own, but all of them."

Our conversation was interrupted by one of my new lady's maids.

"Excuse me," she said. "Ettu, is my lady ready for her bath? The water has been brought and she might wish to bathe while it is still hot."

Ettu looked to me, her eyebrows arched in a way that suggested she found the conversation amusing.

"Well, my lady," she said. "Shall we go have your bath?"

I shrugged and she led me to the corner of the chamber where there was a small alcove I hadn't noticed. It held a chamber pot and a tiled stall with a stool, which I quickly discovered was intended for bathing. They undressed me and I sat on the stool while they poured hot water over me, then scrubbed my body with salt.

My cheeks heated at having to sit there completely naked while they washed me, but it seemed it was only me who felt uncomfortable with it. The women chattered amongst themselves as they worked. At first I tuned them out, because it was too hard to follow the rapid conversations in their own language, but when Ettu cleared her throat, I realised I should be listening.

"And she said Pharaoh gave her a carnelian pendant," one of the women said. "But when Kia asked to see it, she said it was too precious to be viewed by anyone else and she had hidden it away."

"So there is no pendant?" another woman asked, her tone sceptical.

"Kia certainly didn't think so."

"Are we ready to do her hair?"

"I have the razor."

It was only as a woman lifted the razor to my forehead that I realised it was now me they discussed.

"Stop," I said. "What are you doing with that?"

The chatter died.

"Ettu, we have wigs for my lady to wear," the woman holding the razor said. "Very fine ones with hair in any style she could possibly wish for. And if we don't have the style she desires, we can have new wigs made however she wants."

"There is nothing wrong with my hair and I would like to keep it." I pretended I hadn't noticed she didn't speak directly to me. "Thank you."

"But..." The woman's voice trailed away and she looked to Ettu for help.

"My lady," Ettu said. "It is the custom here that all body hair is removed. It makes it easier to keep the body clean and free of insects."

"I don't have insects in my hair." My voice was frosty now.

"Not yet," Ettu said.

"What about you?" I glanced at her hair which was pinned back in a bun as usual. "Do you intend to shave your head?"

"We are doing it tonight," she said. "There was no time this morning, given how long we spent being lectured on protocols."

I looked at the women who surrounded me, suddenly self-conscious again about my nakedness.

"Do you all have shaved heads?" I asked.

They all murmured variations of *of course, my lady* and *yes, my lady.*

"Perhaps we could do it tomorrow?" I said.

Ettu made a noise that told me this wasn't an acceptable suggestion. I wondered whether they would even let me leave the bathing chamber without shaving my head. Despite the fact that everything was supposed to be about catering to my wishes, there seemed much I had no control over.

"Fine then," I said. "Just do it."

"Excellent." Ettu nodded to the woman with the razor and she started scraping it over my scalp.

I closed my eyes as my hair dropped to the floor. I couldn't bear to see it lying there. In Babylon, hair was part of a woman's beauty. I had never in my life thought it might one day be removed from my head. Tears leaked from my eyes and I hoped nobody noticed. They would think me a fool for crying over my hair. Someone's fingers briefly clasped my elbow as if to offer comfort. Ettu most likely. I couldn't imagine any of the other women doing such a thing, even Nammu or Belet-ili. Especially them.

I had thought it would be over once they shaved my head, but apparently that was only the beginning. They shaved every last hair from my body, even in the most intimate places. My arms, my legs, my eyebrows. I said nothing, only let them work, holding out an arm or a leg when they asked me to and acutely conscious of how hot my cheeks were. Although they spoke very respectfully — it was all *would my lady be so kind as to hold out her arm for me* — I knew I had no choice but to submit to their ministrations. I kept my eyes closed the whole time.

Once they finished removing my hair, they rubbed me all over with scented oils. My nose tingled and my eyes itched.

"Do you have something that doesn't smell quite so strong?" I asked.

"Oh, but my lady, this smells delightful," one of the women said.

"I have heard this is Pharaoh's favourite scent," another said. "We will only adorn you in what we know he likes."

So even my own scent was no longer within my control.

They led me back out to the main chamber after that and I was able to open my eyes without seeing my hair all over the floor. The women dressed me in a thin linen tunic that came down to my knees, with a sheer ankle-length gown over the top.

"Why do I need two gowns?" I asked.

"My lady, that is not two gowns," a maid said with a giggle that made me feel like a fool for asking. "The bottom one is your undergown and the one on top is for beauty. Look how thin the fabric is. It is a truly exceptional item."

"I stitched the hem myself," another woman said. "See the tiny lotus flowers? They are so intricate that it took me months to complete."

"It is very beautiful," I said, since she seemed to expect praise.

It wasn't a lie either. Her stitching was extremely fine, better even than Ishtar's, but the detail of my hem seemed unimportant. They had changed everything about me. I no longer looked like a Babylonian. I was no longer myself. I longed to run my hands over my scalp and see if it was really true they had taken every last strand of hair. Was my head smooth or would I be able to feel the remnants of where my hair had been? I had to clasp my hands together to stop myself.

They brought a selection of wigs for me to inspect. The hair pieces were complicated and finely detailed. I looked for one with the style I was accustomed to, a bun set high on the back of my head, but there was nothing so plain. There were wigs with long braids that would dangle halfway down my back. Wigs of tight curls. Wigs with the back sections left to hang loose while the front was pinned up in elaborate styles.

"Ettu, which one would my lady like to wear today?" a maid asked.

Her own hairstyle was much simpler than any of the hair

pieces, with a section of hair brushed forward and fastened with a pretty clip. I couldn't see anything so simple in the selection they offered me.

"That one." I pointed to one of the braided styles. It seemed less fussy than most of the others.

"Oh, a lovely choice," the woman said enthusiastically.

"What is your name?" I asked her.

"Merytre, my lady." She bowed from her waist.

"Have you worked at the Palace for very long?"

"Almost six years." Her voice was proud.

I examined her face. Was she older than she looked? I would have guessed her to be no more than a year or two older than myself. Sixteen at most.

"My mother was an Ornament," she said, perhaps guessing my curiosity. "She died when I was very young, but Panouk let me stay."

Panouk was the man Ettu mentioned, the one in charge of the Palace. He must be senior to Amankhau, who I met last night.

"I am working to pay off the debts I accumulated while I was young," Merytre continued.

How could a child have incurred so much debt?

"I am very grateful to him," she said. "I had nowhere else to go, you see."

"Of course," I said.

I wondered who her father was if her mother had fallen pregnant while she was an Ornament. Did that mean Merytre's father was Pharaoh himself, or had her mother had an affair? I couldn't think of a tactful way to ask, especially in front of the other maids, and I supposed it was none of my business anyway.

I hardly recognised myself when one of the women passed me a hand mirror. They had made up my face with long lines of kohl around my eyes, far more rouge than I would normally wear, and a dark powder on my lips. My shaved eyebrows had been drawn back on.

The wig was almost the same colour as my own hair, so although the styling was different, it didn't look too odd, not to my eye at least. It felt strange to have it press against my scalp, though, and to know there was no hair of my own beneath it. I pushed the thought out of my mind. I didn't want to cry in front of these women and I particularly didn't want to ruin their eye makeup and have to sit here even longer while they reapplied it.

Show Pharaoh what the women of Babylon are made of.

CHAPTER 20

*E*ttu shooed the women out of my chamber when she heard my stomach growl.

"I will show you where you can get something to eat," she said to me.

"Have you seen Tall and Half yet?" I asked.

She shook her head.

"I will ask around," she said. "As long as they found the stables, I am sure they had somewhere to sleep last night."

"It is not just last night I am worried about. What are they to do if they aren't allowed to be here with me? I never would have brought them if I had known."

They would have been better off in Father's court, despite how they were mocked there. At least they had beds and food and clean clothes. They had jobs — Half was a messenger, and Tall fetched and carried things. His limited ability to communicate never interfered with his capacity to understand what someone wanted brought to them or taken somewhere, and he carried even the heaviest items with ease. What would happen to them here? Where would they find work and accommodation?

"I suppose none of us would have come if we had known the situation here," Ettu said.

I guessed she wasn't referring to herself, or to Nammu or Belet-ili, or to Ahmose, since none of them had any choice in whether they accompanied me.

"This was not my choice," I reminded her. "Ishtar was supposed to come, not me."

Would Ishtar have been relegated to the Palace of the Ornaments? Or would the guards at Pharaoh's palace have taken one look at her beautiful face and admitted her? Would Pharaoh have been besotted and taken her as his Great Royal Wife, pushing aside the woman who already held that position? I would never know, but Ishtar definitely would have managed the situation better than I had. My stomach growled again, drawing me from my thoughts.

"Come," Ettu said. "Let's get you some breakfast."

Before we reached the dining chamber, a boy of perhaps eight years raced up and stopped in front of me. He bowed deeply, an unexpectedly elegant movement for a lad of his age. I wondered if he too was modified, as Panouk had said the men were, or if he was too young.

"Are you the Lady Kassaya?" he asked.

"I am."

"Lady Tiye asks that you attend her in her chambers," he said.

The Ornament Ettu had mentioned earlier. The one who was Pharaoh's favourite. Perhaps she intended to welcome me?

"I will go to her once I have eaten," I said. "Thank you."

"My lady, Lady Tiye has summoned you," he said.

Unsure what he expected from me, I looked to Ettu.

"Lady Tiye is the Top Ornament," she said.

I shrugged. "What does that have to do with me?"

The boy shuffled his feet and seemed agitated.

"I suspect," Ettu said. "That when Lady Tiye summons an Ornament, she goes."

The boy heaved a sigh of relief and bowed.

"Shall I tell my lady you are on your way?" he asked.

I hesitated. This was no welcome. It was a strategic move, but I couldn't yet guess Tiye's game. The question was whether to submit, at least until I knew what she wanted, or to take a stand.

"I will go to her after breakfast," I said to the boy. "You may tell her."

He blanched and looked pleadingly at Ettu, obviously hoping she would talk sense into me.

"Go on then," she said to him. "My lady has given her answer."

He bowed again and hurried away.

"Are you sure that was wise?" Ettu asked once he was out of hearing.

"I suppose I will find out," I said.

Ettu led me to a sumptuous chamber, where several women dressed much like me already sat on thick cushions, each beside a low table of her own. Servants — all female — bustled around, bringing mugs and platters to the seated women. I hesitated in the doorway as everyone looked at me. *Show Pharaoh what the women of Babylon are made of.*

"Good morning," I said.

"Well, well," one of the women said. She made a show of eyeing me up and down. "Look what we have here."

"I am Kassaya," I said. "Princess of Babylon."

"No longer," she said. "You are now an Ornament of Pharaoh. I trust you know what that means."

I didn't want to look foolish in front of these women.

"Of course," I said smoothly.

"You look like you're taking it better than most of us did when we arrived." She pointed to a cushion near hers. "Sit."

As much as I longed to ask what she meant, I kept my mouth closed. I would use this opportunity to learn what I could without revealing my ignorance. I lowered myself to the cushion, trying to move as gracefully as I could, aware of their eyes on me, and tucked my legs to the side in the manner of the other women. The table held only a small bowl of water and a linen towel, which I assumed was intended for hand washing.

Ettu crouched beside me to fuss with my skirt, straightening it so the fabric wouldn't wrinkle, then retreated to stand with her back against the wall where several other women waited, presumably lady's maids to other Ornaments.

A serving woman brought a tray of mugs.

"Beer, milk, or melon juice, my lady?" she asked.

"Milk," I said. "Please."

She set a mug on the table beside me and hurried away.

I tasted my drink and found it to be warm goat milk. I had taken no more than a single sip before another serving woman appeared.

"Bread, my lady?" She lowered the tray to show me an assortment of breads. There was both flat bread and bread risen with yeast. Brown bread, white bread, grainy bread.

"That one," I said, pointing, and she handed me a thick chunk of brown bread.

Another serving woman appeared with small pots of honey and slabs of butter, followed by one with wedges of cheese. I took both honey and cheese, before yet another woman brought a tray of dates and figs. I waved her away, my mouth already full of bread and honey. My nose still ran from the scented oil my lady's maids had rubbed all over me and I tried not to sniffle as I ate.

"Have you met Tiye yet?" the Ornament who had greeted me asked.

I had almost forgotten the other women in my hurry to eat. I chewed my bread carefully before I swallowed, not wanting to choke and make a fool of myself.

"I have not," I said. "But I have received a message to go to her chamber."

"And you came here instead?"

I couldn't interpret her voice, but her face seemed to show grudging admiration.

"I was hungry," I said.

A couple of the other Ornaments tittered.

"She will make you pay for that," one said.

She was quickly shushed by another.

"Why would it matter to Tiye whether I went straight away or ate first?" I asked. "Yesterday was a long day and I didn't have any dinner. Surely she can wait a little."

The Ornament who had been speaking to me only shook her head.

"You will see," she said.

"Tell me your name," I said. "I gave you mine."

"Henutmire," she said. "Daughter of Sanakht."

I nodded and hoped she wouldn't realise I didn't know her father if that was her expectation. She looked to be of Egyptian birth so perhaps he was well known. I glanced around the room.

"And the rest of you?" I asked.

"Ineni," said a woman who also looked to be Egyptian.

"Gilukhipa," said another whose paler skin marked her as a foreigner compared to the other women, although she didn't look all that different from me. "From Mitanni."

"Nebtu," said the last. Like everyone except Gilukhipa, she looked to be of Egyptian stock.

I bowed my head towards each as they were introduced. Were they noble women? Gilukhipa might even be a princess, given she was from another country. Perhaps, like me, she was sent to seal an alliance, only to discover Pharaoh already had other wives. I wondered whether any of these women might become friends. Gilukhipa seemed to give me a friendly smile, but I couldn't read the others.

The servant women brought around their trays again, but I declined any more food. As I dipped my fingers in the bowl of water and wiped them on the cloth, Ettu appeared at my side.

"My lady, if you are ready?" she said.

My sandals tangled in my skirt as I rose and I stumbled, almost falling on top of my little table. Somebody laughed, but the sound died abruptly. I wondered who had glared her into silence and why.

Ettu made me wait while she straightened my clothing. My cheeks were hot and I wanted nothing more than to run from the chamber, but that would look even less elegant than I had already shown myself to be.

"I have found out where Lady Tiye's chamber is," Ettu said. "Come, I will take you there."

I waited until we left the dining chamber before I spoke.

"Have you learned anything else about Tiye?" I asked, wondering what the comment about her making me pay meant, but Ettu shook her head. I supposed I would find out soon enough.

It was quite a long walk to Tiye's chamber and two flights of stairs. My legs were still tired from yesterday and my feet hurt. My lady's maids had wrapped my feet in linen bandages, tutting over the spots where my sandals had rubbed right through my skin. The bandages eased the pain somewhat, but it still hurt to walk.

"I believe this is her wing." Ettu slowed as we approached a branching corridor. She pointed to the left where a pair of double doors stood at the end of a long hallway.

"She has a whole wing?" And I had thought my bedchamber was luxurious.

"I will wait here for you. Apparently she allows only her own lady's maids inside her chamber and nobody else is to even enter her wing without invitation."

I set off down the hallway. My heart thudded and I felt unaccountably nervous. She was just another Ornament, I told myself. Just a woman like me. There was no reason to be nervous. But the laughter in the dining chamber had made me uneasy.

I reached the doors and knocked. They were made of a dark wood, polished until they shone, and carved with a pattern of twisting vines. The door opened and a woman peered out at me. This couldn't be Tiye. Her gown and wig were too plain. She must be a lady's maid.

"I am here to see Tiye," I said.

The door closed.

Had I misunderstood? The messenger boy said I should come to her chambers. Before I could decide what to do, the door opened again.

"She will see you now," the woman said and stood aside so I could enter.

Tiye's chamber was easily four times the size of mine and had tapestries and soft rugs which were clearly of higher quality than mine. Doorways positioned at intervals around the room revealed this was no more than a single chamber within a suite. It seemed my chamber was not as fine as I thought. Next to Tiye's, it looked almost insultingly small and plain.

Tiye lay on a long couch beneath a window, her back propped up with cushions. A low table beside her bore the remains of her breakfast. She, it seemed, did not eat in the dining chamber with the other Ornaments. How many other women had their meals brought to their chambers? There were supposed to be several hundred Ornaments, yet I had dined with only four this morning. I supposed there must be many dining chambers to accommodate so many wives as Pharaoh apparently had.

"So." Tiye gave me a hard stare as if she had already found me wanting. She was perhaps a dozen years older than me and her face bore evidence of a heritage that was only partially Egyptian. "You finally deigned to present yourself to me."

"I was hungry and couldn't think of anything that would be so urgent as to require my presence before I ate."

Her stare turned cold and I already regretted my hasty words.

"Has anyone told you how things work around here?" she asked.

I kept my mouth closed and only shook my head. I detected an undertone of malice in her voice and suspected anything I had learned about the Palace was not what she referred to.

"As the newest girl to arrive, you have the honour of cleaning my bathing chamber," Tiye said.

"I… what?"

"It is that way." She pointed, then nodded to her lady's maid. "You may show her."

"This way please." The woman led me to a doorway which opened onto a bathing chamber that was twice the size of mine.

"Oh, phew." I held my hand over my nose to block the stench of urine. My eyes burned.

The maid pointed to a mop and bucket in the corner.

"You should be here by dawn every morning," she said. "Scrub it well and you will give her no cause to make it any harder for you."

"This must be a joke."

She gave me a look that suggested she almost felt sorry for me.

"The newest Ornament always cleans my lady's bathing chamber," she said. "Pray to whichever god you worship that some other woman arrives soon to save you from it."

She scurried away.

Like mine, Tiye's bathing chamber comprised a tiled area and a separate bathing stall with a stool. Unlike mine, it also held an overflowing chamber pot. The entire floor outside the bathing stall was covered in yellow liquid.

"What did you do? Save all your piss for a week?" I muttered to myself.

This was ridiculous. I marched back out to Tiye, but she was gone. Fine, I would leave. Let her own serving women clean up her mess. I wouldn't do it. But when I tried to open the door to the hallway, it was locked. I rapped on it.

"Is anyone there?" I called.

"I am sorry, my lady." It sounded like the woman who had shown me the bathing chamber. "I am not permitted to let you out until you have finished cleaning."

"Don't be absurd," I said. "Let me out of here at once."

She didn't reply.

I banged on the door with my fists.

"Let me out," I called.

Still no reply.

The administrator. Surely he wouldn't stand for such a thing.

"I demand to speak with Panouk," I called.

"Nobody comes down this hallway but my lady's own servants," the woman said. "And it is not worth our positions to help you. I am sorry, I truly am, but the sooner you do what she says, the sooner I can let you out."

"This is illegal," I called and pounded on the door again. "You cannot lock me in here and refuse to let me out."

"A word of warning, my lady." Her voice was lower now and I stopped my pounding in order to hear her. "My lady is Pharaoh's most favoured Ornament. He listens to her. She can make your life very, very difficult if you cross her. You could be thrown out of the Palace, sentenced to servitude."

"My father is Marduk-apla-iddina of Babylon. He made an alliance with Pharaoh. He will not stand for his daughter being treated like this. I will write to him the moment I am released from here."

"Such a letter will never leave the Palace, my lady." Her voice was almost sympathetic now. "The scribe Pentau controls all correspondence. He and he alone decides what may be sent. Your letters to your father will never be anything but glowing accounts of your life here."

The seriousness of my situation finally became clear. I was locked in Tiye's chambers until I did what she demanded of me. I was confined to the Palace unless Pharaoh decided to let me out. I couldn't even send a letter unless the scribe approved its contents.

I supposed I could clean Tiye's bathroom and be done with it. But then she would expect me back here to do it again tomorrow, and the day after, and the day after that. If I did it even once, just to buy me time to figure out how to avoid it in future, it would be that much harder to get out of it the next time. Tiye's goal was obviously to humiliate me. The decision I needed to make was whether I would allow her to do so.

Whether or not she knew I was a princess, or that I was sent to fulfil an alliance, she certainly knew I was an Ornament. Surely that should mean I was treated with some measure of respect.

Show Pharaoh what the women of Babylon are made of.

I would be sent back to my father in disgrace before I would clean Tiye's bathroom for her. I needed to find a way out of her chambers.

CHAPTER 21

started with the windows. Tiye's chambers were on the third floor, but perhaps there was a tree growing conveniently nearby or some other means by which I could climb out. Unfortunately, her windows were all situated for perfect views of the gardens with nothing to obscure them. I studied the distance to the ground, but determined it was too far to be sure I wouldn't badly injure myself, at the least, if I jumped.

Maybe I could lever the door open. I searched her chests and drawers. Tiye had all manner of cosmetics and perfumes, oils and unguents, jewels, gems and beads, but nothing useful. Nothing sturdy with a pointed end I might wedge between the door and its frame. As I rummaged through her things, I wondered why she gave me such easy access to them. I couldn't be the first woman who had searched her chambers for a means of escape.

So it seemed my options were to either wait — Tiye would want to return to her chambers eventually — or to find a way out a window. I returned to the windows, hoping to spot Tall and Half. They would help me if they knew I was trapped in here. They might have to fetch the administrator, or even the police chief, but they would do something. Perhaps when I didn't return, Ettu would go to them for help.

I watched absently as a man made his way around the gardens, keeping to the perimeter as he traced a path beside the high walls. Like Khaemmalu, he wore a shirt with the standard *shendyt* and sandals, so maybe he was a guard. When he cut through the grounds heading towards the Palace, I took my chance.

"Hello there," I called once he was within earshot.

His gaze went straight to me. So, he had already noticed me at the window, even though I hadn't seen him look towards me before. He gave me a half bow and kept walking.

"I am Kassaya," I called.

"Sutempiamana," he called back. "You can call me Sutem."

"Do you think you can help me, Sutem?"

"What is the problem?"

"I am trapped in these chambers and the door seems to be locked. I cannot get out."

He studied me for a moment.

"It would seem the chambers in which you are trapped belong to Lady Tiye," he said.

"Is that so? I wandered in here by mistake and the door must have blown closed."

"And I assume the door somehow locked itself after it blew closed?"

"That must be the case." I tried to sound cheery and unconcerned. He at least seemed to be considering helping me. "If I was to climb out the window, is there a way I could get down safely?"

"Not from those windows unless you are an especially talented climber."

"What if I had a rope?" I asked. "And someone who could pull me up from the roof?"

"That might be possible, assuming you could find a rope and someone to help you."

"I don't suppose you would do that?"

"Regretfully, my lady, I cannot. I am not permitted inside the Palace and there is no way to get to the roof other than from inside. My task is to protect you from out here."

"You couldn't sneak inside? Just this once?"

"I apologise, but no. It wouldn't be merely my job I lost if I was caught."

"What do you mean?"

"I would be executed."

I gaped at him.

"Just for entering the Palace?"

"For entering the Palace as an unmodified man."

"Unmodified? I have heard that word before, but nobody has explained what it means."

"Aah, my lady, this is probably a conversation best had when we are not shouting from such a distance."

"I see." I didn't really. "Is there something else you can do?"

"It seems to me you need help from within the Palace. Somebody you trust."

"There is someone I trust, although she isn't in here with me and I don't have a way of getting a message to her."

"I have some rope. She could take it up onto the roof, tie the end on up there and let it dangle down in front of your window. Then you could climb down."

"How would she get access to the roof?" I asked.

"She simply goes up the stairs. Nobody will stop her. We often sleep on our roofs when it is a particularly hot night."

"Would you be able to get a message to her?"

"I can try. If she is in your chamber, I might be able to get her attention without anyone else noticing."

"I don't know if she is there."

"I will see."

He started to walk away.

"Wait," I called. "Don't you need to know where my chamber is?"

"I already know," he said.

I leaned against the windowsill while I waited. It must be late morning by now and the day was already hot. Sweat trickled down my back, but I didn't want to leave the window and risk missing Sutem if he returned.

From this height, I could just see over the wall, although the view would be better from the level above. What I could see of Thebes looked much the same as any other Egyptian town we had sailed past on our way here. Mud brick buildings, tall palm trees. There was little else I could see with the wall in the way.

After some time, a rope suddenly appeared beside me. I leaned out and peered up to the roof, and could only just see Ettu's face as she leaned over, two floors above me. She waved and continued to let down the rope. By the time it reached the ground, Sutem had returned. Now the moment had come, I doubted whether I could do it.

"I don't know," I said to Sutem. "What if I can't hold on tightly enough?"

"Do you have something to wrap around your hands? Perhaps a length of linen? That will protect your skin and also help you grip the rope better."

"Wait a moment."

I rummaged through Tiye's clothing chests until I found a flimsy nightgown which looked delicate enough for me to rip in half. I used a hair pin to tear a hole in the seam, then tugged. The fabric tore with a satisfying noise.

"Sorry, Tiye," I muttered. "I do hope that wasn't too expensive."

I wrapped the fabric around my palms, tucking in the ends and hoping they would stay in place long enough. At the window, I held out my hands to show Sutem.

"That will do it," he said. "The tricky part will be getting out the window. Get yourself up so you are sitting on the windowsill."

I dragged a stool over to the window and used it to climb up. With my skirts hiked up to my thighs, I straddled the sill. My heart pounded and I paused to steady my breath. If I fell now, I would die. Maybe I should just clean Tiye's gods-damned bathroom? No, I couldn't let her win. Marduk only knew what she would do next if I didn't stand up to her this time. Then I was sitting on the sill with both legs outside. I clutched the window frame and tried to catch my breath.

"Good," Sutem said. "Now grab the rope and put it between your feet. That's it. Just tuck one foot over the other with the rope between them. It will help you control your descent."

I didn't like the way that sounded. Control your descent. It suggested something that might easily become uncontrolled.

"Hold on tightly," Sutem said. "Keep your feet close together. Now you're going to slip off the window sill and let the rope take your weight."

I clutched the rope and breathed shakily. Beneath the linen wrappings, my palms were sweating.

"Come on," he said. "Just slide off."

Keep breathing. In and out.

"Any time now," he said.

"I can't." My body wouldn't move.

"You must fight the fear. Or you can sit there all day. Your choice."

I didn't want to be sitting in her window when Tiye returned. I took a deep breath and counted to three. But I got to three and kept sitting there.

"Come on," Sutem said. "I can't help you do it. The only one who can do this is you."

I gripped the rope tighter. My head spun. What if I fainted and fell off the windowsill?

"It is only a little way," Sutem said. "Hardly anything at all. Just hold tight and slide off."

"I can't."

"I am afraid I have work to do." He started walking away. "As pleasant as it has been, I can't stand here all day."

"Wait," I called, but he didn't stop. "Sutem."

With another deep breath, I clutched the rope as hard as I could and slid off the window.

"Sutem," I shrieked.

But I didn't fall.

"Good," came Sutem's voice. I didn't let myself look down. "Now let your feet slide apart just a tiny bit and lean back."

My arms already trembled from exhaustion. When I moved my feet, I started sliding down the rope.

"Sutem."

My descent was faster than I anticipated and all of a sudden, I reached the grass, landing so hard my legs buckled.

"I told you you could do it," he said.

"You could have caught me," I grumbled as I got to my feet.

The linen around my hands was shredded, but the skin of my palms barely had any scrapes. I straightened my gown, brushed off a few blades of grass, and glared at Sutem. He only shrugged.

"I am not permitted to touch an Ornament," he said. "Not unless she is in mortal danger and there is no other way to save her life. It is another one of those things that would cost far more than my job."

It reminded me of his earlier comment.

"Now will you tell me what it means to be modified?" I asked.

He cleared his throat and looked away for a moment.

"It means a man who has had certain... body parts removed. To ensure he can be physically near the Ornaments without temptation."

"You mean..."

He cleared his throat again.

"And you haven't…"

"The guards who patrol the grounds are not modified," he said. "And that is why we are not permitted inside."

"Because you might…"

"Well, I wouldn't. I know the rules and I don't particularly want to lose either my job or my life. But Pharaoh takes no chances when it comes to the safety of his Ornaments."

Personally, I thought Pharaoh sounded like the jealous type. This wasn't about protecting his precious Ornaments who were locked in the Palace and allowed no outside contact without approval. It was about ensuring the Ornaments were dependant on him. For everything.

"Why did you help me then?" I asked. "Could it get you in trouble?"

"Certainly, although not as much trouble as if I had touched you."

But he hadn't answered my question.

"So why?" I asked again.

Sutem gave me a steady look.

"Now you are in my debt," he said. "There might come a day when I will need a favour from someone within the Palace. I will expect you to return my aid."

CHAPTER 22

My feet were slow as I made my way to the front doors. This place was nothing like I had expected. I had been separated from two of my companions, humiliated by another Ornament, and it was quite clear I would never be queen. I hadn't even met Pharaoh yet. But what choice did I have other than to try to make a life for myself here?

If I wanted to flee, I was almost certain Ettu and Ahmose would come with me. But we didn't know where Tall and Half were, and I couldn't leave without them. They were only here because of me. And where would we go anyway? Even if I could get to Babylon, Father would probably send me straight back to Egypt. He wouldn't risk breaking the alliance, no matter how much his disobedient daughter begged to be released. I was trapped. It seemed my only option was to make the best of the situation I had been sent to.

I expected to introduce myself to the guards at the entrance since they probably weren't the same men who admitted me last night, but they already held the doors open. Maybe they assumed a lone woman walking through the grounds dressed as I was must be an Ornament and entitled to enter the Palace.

"Good morning," I said to them. "I am Kassaya. I arrived last night from Babylon."

Surprise flickered across their faces. Maybe they weren't used to Ornaments introducing themselves. But if I was to survive here, I needed allies. And allies who could facilitate my getting in and out of the Palace would be valuable indeed.

"Khaemope, my lady," one of them said. He gestured to his companion. "He is Karpusa."

"Khaemope and Karpusa," I repeated, fixing their names and faces in my mind. "I am most pleased to meet you. Are you always at the doors during the day?"

"We are the day shift," Khaemope said. "We come on at dawn."

"Do you wish to go inside, my lady?" Karpusa asked.

I finally realised they were still holding open the doors.

"Yes," I said. "But before I do, have you seen two Babylonian men this morning? A tall one and a very short one?"

They both stiffened.

"Of course not, my lady," Karpusa said, or maybe he was Khaemope. "They would not get through the front gates, and even if they did we have guards patrolling the grounds constantly. They would be found before they could be of any threat to you."

"Oh, no, you misunderstand me," I said. "They are my companions. They travelled with me from Babylon, but they weren't permitted to enter the Palace. They were sent to sleep in the stables, but I haven't seen them since then."

"I'm afraid they would not have been allowed to stay in the stables," Khaemope said.

"The administrator said they could spend the night there," I said. "Amankhau, I think his name was."

"And do you know for a fact they reached the stables?" Karpusa asked.

"Well, no, but a man was to take them there."

The guards darted glances at each other and Karpusa shook his head slightly.

"What is it?" I asked.

My heart pounded. Did they know something? Had something happened to Tall and Half?

"I am sorry to say it, but even if Amankhau told you they would be permitted to stay overnight, they would have been turned out immediately," Karpusa said. "Pharaoh has decreed no man may enter the Palace unless approved by himself. I am not sure how they even got in the gates. The night guards have likely already been removed."

"For merely letting my companions see me as far as the front doors? Surely not."

He only shrugged.

"Rules are rules," he said. "Pharaoh takes the security of his Ornaments very seriously. We all know the rules when we take these jobs."

"And my companions? What would have happened to them?"

"If the gate guards admitted letting them in, they might have been merely turned out," Khaemope said. "If the guards denied it…"

His voice trailed away. I could only stare at him, speechless. Dear Marduk. Don't let the mere fact that Tall and Half walked through those gates with me mean they lost their lives.

"Why would the guards let them in then?" I asked. "Why didn't they refuse?"

One of them had said men weren't allowed in, but I insisted. If something had happened to them, it was my fault.

Both men shrugged.

"We cannot say, my lady," Karpusa said.

"I need to go to my chamber." I didn't think I could trust myself to speak further without crying.

Karpusa gestured for me to enter and I swept past them without another word. My only thought was that I had to find

Ettu and Ahmose, so we could come up with a plan to locate Tall and Half. If they were still alive.

I found my chamber with only one wrong turn. I hadn't paid much attention last night, not expecting to navigate the hallways alone so soon. I burst through the door, closed it behind me, and leaned against it as I cried.

"My lady? Are you injured? Did I not tie the rope securely enough?"

I didn't notice Ettu until she spoke. Unable to talk through my sobs, I could only shake my head.

"I couldn't see your descent," she said. "Did you fall? Have you twisted your ankle?"

"Tall and Half," I finally managed. "Have you found them?"

"I have asked around, but nobody has word of them. I was waiting to see you return in case you needed something else and then I was planning to go to the stables myself. But tell me what happened? Why did you need to climb out the window?"

My tears subsided as I told her about being locked in Tiye's suite until I cleaned her urine-soaked bathing chamber. Ettu's face was suitably horrified.

"She cannot treat you like that," she said. "You should lodge a complaint with the administrator."

"I'm not sure that is a good idea," I said. "Apparently Tiye has Pharaoh's ear and he does what she asks of him. She could make a lot of trouble for me."

"Sounds like the type to make up lies too. Whatever she tells Pharaoh probably isn't the truth, or not the whole truth anyway. She might even be able to have you turned out of the Palace."

"I'm not so sure that would be a bad thing." My tone was grim and she looked alarmed.

"What else have you heard?" she asked.

I relayed my conversation with the door guards. Ettu put her hand over her mouth and shook her head.

"Surely not," she whispered. "What kind of person would order two men killed for merely entering the grounds?"

"They said it would depend on whether the gate guards admitted letting them in. I suppose if they denied it, it makes it seem like Tall and Half snuck in somehow."

"I will go straight to the stables," Ettu said. "And make sure they are safe. What do I tell them if they are there, though? Where do they go?"

"Just tell them to get out of here and find accommodation nearby. I need time to think. I will get a message out to them as soon as I can."

"How?" Ettu asked. "We already know you cannot send a message except through the Palace scribe and he will hardly allow you to communicate with two unknown men if what we have heard is correct."

"I will think of something."

Ahmose might be able to help. She said she knew secret things. I needed to find out what they were.

"Go to the stables and make sure they are safe," I said. "Then find Ahmose."

CHAPTER 23

Ahmose rapped on my door long before Ettu returned. I led her to the couch beneath the window. We sat and Ahmose looked at me expectantly. I didn't know how to start the conversation about what I needed to know.

"Have you been given suitable accommodation?" I asked instead.

"I am sharing a chamber with three other women," she said. "It seems nobody knows what to do with me. From what I have heard, it is rather unusual for an Ornament to bring someone with her who is not a maid or personal servant."

"What did you tell them?"

"That I was your tutor. It didn't seem like a lie."

"No, that's good. Hopefully that will mean they don't assign you any other tasks. You must tell me if they do, so I can try to get you out of them."

Ahmose was far too old to suffer helping with cleaning or washing or whatever else women who lived in the Palace did if they were not maids or serving women.

"Have you heard anything that might be useful to me?" I asked.

"I am hearing lots of things. An old woman like me, she is mostly invisible to the young ones who parade down the hallways. They don't watch their tongues in front of an old woman."

"Tell me."

"There is a woman called Naparaye who is with child. She claims the father is Pharaoh, but it seems not everyone is convinced of that."

"Who else could it be? No men are permitted in here unless they are modified and from what I have gleaned, I think that means they wouldn't be able to get a woman with child."

"But the guards who patrol the grounds are not modified." She gave me an arch look. "It seems Pharaoh believes the men who physically protect his Ornaments must be whole in order to be strong enough to keep danger from entering these doors."

"So she had an affair with a guard?"

Was it one of those I had already met? Sutem, who helped me this morning, or Khaemmalu, who thought I was flirting with him last night? My cheeks heated again at the memory. Marduk, let it not be Khaemmalu! That would make it seem even worse if he thought I was flirting. He might think I, too, wanted an affair with him.

Ahmose gave me a curious look as if she had noticed my blushing, but if she wondered at it, she kept her thoughts to herself.

"I have also heard Lady Tiye likes to make sure all new Ornaments are well aware of both her position and theirs," she said instead.

"Apparently she makes the newest Ornament scrub her bathing chamber after she has pissed all over it," I said. "Or at least she tries to."

"She has already sent for you?"

"She had her lady's maid lock me in her chambers. I climbed out the window."

Ahmose looked like she didn't know whether to laugh or admonish me.

"I don't think she will give up easily," she warned. "From what I have heard of her, she is a woman who gets what she wants."

"But if what she wants is for me to clean her bathing chamber, she won't get it this time. Especially now I know how to get out. But I called you here to discuss something else. On the ship you said you could teach me secret things. I need to know what sort of things you meant."

She gave me a guarded look.

"All sorts of things, Princess," she said. "Esoteric knowledge. Rare things. Forbidden things."

"Where did you learn such knowledge?"

"From my mother, and her mother. Other women I have met on my journey through life."

"Did you kill the man you were given to?"

She looked me right in the eyes. "Yes."

"How?"

"I dosed him with a certain herb. Just a little in his evening meal every night for a week. He fell ill, then he began vomiting. Soon enough, he died."

"Nobody suspected you?"

"They might have, had I given him a larger dose. If he was perfectly well and then suddenly dead, folk might ask questions. But when a man becomes gradually sicker and sicker, nobody suspects the servant who looks after him and patiently cleans up his vomit when he doesn't even try to get it in a bucket."

"Why did you do it?" I asked.

"He was a cruel man. And I didn't intend to be treated as his possession any longer."

"Tell me what other things you know. You have been very secretive and I need to know whether you can be useful for me."

"Tell me what you want to know," she countered. "I know so many things that I could hardly list them all off."

"I need to get a letter out of the Palace. Maybe several letters."

"That hardly requires esoteric knowledge. There is a scribe who will transcribe your letters for you and ensure they are sent."

"He will also amend the message if he thinks it unsuitable."

"You want to send a letter without anyone else knowing?" Ahmose tapped her chin as she considered the problem. "I may have a way of achieving that. It could be dangerous, though. If you are caught…"

"I expect there would be some kind of punishment."

Could it be any worse than what Tiye had tried to subject me to this morning?

"I need to gather some things," Ahmose said. "It may take me a day or two to locate what I need since I have no trusted suppliers here yet. In the meantime, you should prepare your letter. Do you have writing instruments?"

"No, you will need to get me some."

"I will find them while I locate the ingredients for the spell."

When Ahmose had hinted at knowing secret things, I hadn't expected spells. I thought she meant knowledge of herbs and such. But a spell was a different matter. For just a moment, I hesitated. Would the punishment be more severe if I was caught not only sending an unauthorised letter, but using a spell to do so? There was no other choice. I needed to make Father aware of what he had sent me to.

"Get your things," I said.

Ahmose bowed and left. I could barely contain my nerves as I waited for Ettu to return. Surely the fact it was taking her so long meant she had learned something about Tall and Half. If they were not in the stables and nobody had seen them, she would have been there and back within the hour. When the door finally opened and Ettu slipped in, I jumped up from my chair. She gave me a startled look, as if she expected me to pounce on her.

"I'm afraid I don't have good news," she said before I could ask. "There was nobody in the stables who could confirm they were there last night."

"They never made it?"

Dismay filled me. I had believed they would be safe. Amankhau said they could sleep there and he sent a man to show them the way. I trusted him.

"What will you do?" she asked.

My mind whirled and for a moment, I couldn't think at all. I stared at the mosaic floor, although I saw nothing of its intricate design. I breathed and tried to steady myself. I would be of no use to Tall and Half if I panicked.

"There is no point in confronting Amankhau," I said. "He will only deny it and say we saw him send them to the stables. And perhaps it is better if he doesn't know we know, not yet anyway."

Slowly my thoughts became clearer.

"We need to know whether they left the Palace grounds," I said. "Go speak to the gate guards. If Tall and Half didn't leave through the gates, they must still be within the grounds. From what I have heard, the gates are the only exit."

"Have you considered…" Ettu's voice trailed away, but I knew where her thoughts had gone.

"I don't believe they would have been harmed." I sounded more certain than I felt. Khaemope and Karpusa were surely wrong. Nobody would execute two men who didn't even know they weren't supposed to be here, not after they were permitted to enter the grounds, and not after I had insisted they accompany me. "Amankhau must know he would get no compliance from me if they were."

"He might count on you not finding out. After all, once you learned you couldn't send or receive private messages, you would probably assume all was well with them, even if they didn't contact you."

"But Amankhau doesn't know everything," I said.

She raised her eyebrows at me. "What do you know that he doesn't?"

I hesitated. She was, after all, my servant. She wasn't a friend.

"You can trust me," she said as if she knew exactly what I was thinking. "I swore to be your ally until you delivered Pharaoh a son. I cannot help you if I don't know your plans."

"Ahmose has a way of getting a letter out," I said. "She needs to make some arrangements, but once everything is ready, I will be able to send a message without risk of it being censored."

"A letter to your father?"

"He needs to know what is happening here. I am sure he never would have sent me if he knew I would be merely an Ornament and not Queen. He certainly wouldn't have sent me to a place where I would be locked away and not even allowed to write my own letters."

"Your father made a treaty with an ally," Ettu said. "Can you be sure this isn't what he agreed to?"

I wasn't sure, despite my words. Father's duty to Babylon was everything to him. If these were the terms for an alliance with Egypt and nothing else could be negotiated, he would have agreed. But surely he would have told me. If he had known, he wouldn't have sent me here unawares. Unless he had told Ishtar and then came to regret it when she found a way out.

"This is not what Father thought he was sending me to," I said. "But Tall and Half are my more immediate concern. We need to know they are safe."

"They could be very useful for you if they made it outside and Ahmose has a way to get messages to them."

"I agree, but we need to know they are safe before we make any other plans."

"I will go speak with the guards," she said. "If Half and Tall left at dawn, the day guards should have already been on duty."

"Go see what you can find out," I said. "Come back as soon as you learn anything."

CHAPTER 24

*E*ttu had been gone for only moments before Merytre arrived. I expected the rest of my lady's maids to follow her in, but it seemed she had come alone.

"Oh, my lady," she said. "I heard about what happened. Lady Tiye is furious."

In my concern for Tall and Half, I had almost forgotten the problem of Tiye and her ridiculous demand.

"Her maid has been dismissed and sent from the Palace in disgrace," Merytre said. "Lady Tiye is sure she opened the door and let you out. I heard a different story, though." She gave me a sly look. "I heard you were seen dangling from a rope outside her window."

I shrugged.

"I am sure all sorts of rumours circulate in a place like this," I said.

Someone rapped firmly on the door.

"And so it begins," Merytre said. "Would you like me to answer the door?"

The knock sounded again.

"You may as well," I said. "I don't expect they will just go away when nobody answers."

Merytre cracked the door open a little.

"Lady Tiye *demands* Lady Kassaya attend her in her chambers immediately," a shrill female voice said.

"I will pass your message on when I see my lady," Merytre said calmly.

"Let me in," the voice said. "My lady bid me search Lady Kassaya's chambers to be sure she wasn't hiding in there."

"I'm sure you can appreciate that I cannot let you in while my lady is not present," Merytre said. "I would lose my position for allowing such an intrusion."

"I demand entry!"

"You can assure Lady Tiye I will let my lady know she is looking for her as soon as I see her."

"That will not be acceptable to my lady. I will lose my position if I return without confirming she is not in there."

"I suppose this is farewell then," Merytre said. "I wish you the luck of the gods."

She closed the door and slid the bar in place to lock it. When she turned back to me, she was grinning.

"I never liked her anyway," she said.

"Merytre, I do believe you rather enjoyed yourself there."

"I always get assigned to the new Ornament," she said with a shrug. She was obviously trying to look unbothered, but I could tell this upset her. "Once a lady has been here for a while, she chooses her favourite maids and dismisses the others. By then, there's always a new Ornament who needs lady's maids and I get reassigned. They're always the same though: meek, vapid women who don't have a thought in their heads other than how to get themselves near to Pharaoh. You're the first one that seems different."

I made a quick decision to trust her.

"Be cautious of what you say around Nammu and Belet-ili," I said. "You can trust Ettu, but not them."

Merytre nodded gravely.

"Thank you, my lady," she said. "And in case it needs to be said, you can trust me."

"Then I will make you this offer," I said. "Serve me well until I bear Pharaoh a son and then if you wish to be released, I will ensure you have sufficient funds to make a new life for yourself."

Surprise flickered across her face, although I saw the way she tried to control it.

"I warn you, though," I said. "I expect absolute loyalty. Give me any reason to suspect treachery from you and I will ensure you are dismissed from the Palace."

Merytre took a moment to consider my words before she dropped to her belly on the floor.

"I assume that is a yes," I said.

"Yes, my lady." Her voice was muffled.

"You can get up." I waited while she got to her feet. "Now, what do I do about Tiye? I assume she won't just give up when I don't answer her summons."

"It isn't likely. I don't think there has ever been an Ornament who has refused her before."

"So I need a way to appease her pride."

"Is there something you can offer her?" she asked.

Before I could answer, someone else knocked on the door.

"My lady's chests have arrived." A male voice and one I didn't recognise.

"Who is that, Merytre?" I asked.

She opened the door to reveal a man who appeared to be in his mid twenties. Like most of the men here, he was shaved bald and wore only a *shendyt* and sandals. I might have called him handsome if he wasn't so puffed up with his own importance. He bowed to me.

"My lady, my name is Panouk," he said. "Chief administrator and at your service."

His voice was smooth and I took an instant dislike to him.

"Good," I said. "I want to lodge a complaint about Amankhau. When I arrived last night, he said my male companions could spend the night in the stables. However, this morning I hear they never arrived there and nobody has heard from them."

"Unfortunately men are not permitted within the Palace of the Ornaments," Panouk said. "Amankhau reported their arrival to me and they were asked to depart at first light."

"Except they never made it to the stables."

"I fear you must be mistaken. The head groom has already reported to me this morning and he assures me they slept comfortably before leaving at dawn."

I didn't know what to believe. Was there any possibility Ettu had misunderstood? Or that whoever her information came from was mistaken?

"I would like to speak with the gate guards," I said. "The ones that let them out this morning."

"I'm afraid that won't be possible. The guards are not permitted inside the Palace and they cannot leave their station during their shift."

"Then I will go to them."

"It is really not necessary."

"If they saw my companions leave this morning, I want to hear it directly from them."

Panouk gave a heavy sigh as if I was being unreasonable.

"I will arrange for somebody to escort you to them," he said. "Would that be acceptable to you?"

And in the meantime, he would likely speak to them himself to make sure they told me what he wanted them to.

"That will be satisfactory." He didn't need to know I had already sent Ettu to the guards.

"Is there anything else you need? I trust your accommodations are suitable?"

How would Tiye respond? I doubted she would say that yes, her chamber was just fine if she knew someone else had a bigger one.

"I'm pleased you asked," I said. "I was in Tiye's chambers this morning and I noticed how much larger than mine they are."

"Well, yes," he spluttered. "Lady Tiye has been here for a long time and she is Pharaoh's Favourite. You see—"

I cut him off.

"My Father would be most unhappy to learn I have been given such a small chamber," I said. "Especially when Tiye has an entire wing to herself. It is really quite insulting to find myself confined to such a small space."

"We can of course move you to alternative chambers." Although his words were still smooth, his face showed his reluctance. "Nothing is too much trouble for an Ornament."

"See to it that this happens today," I said. "I don't expect to spend another night in this horrid place. Now, if we are done?"

Merytre was already waiting at the door to let him out.

Panouk spluttered but couldn't seem to find his words and he left without whatever objection he wanted to make. Merytre closed the door firmly behind him.

"I don't believe I have ever heard of an Ornament demanding larger chambers before." Her tone was admiring. "And I certainly haven't ever heard of someone asking outright why Lady Tiye has better chambers than she does."

I doubted Tiye got her suite by doing anything other than demanding it. It seemed there were games to be played if one wanted to get ahead in this place. I would have to learn them quickly.

CHAPTER 25

Within the hour, I was ensconced in my new suite on the third floor, right next to the hallway which led to Tiye's chambers. As I arrived, the last of my chests were being brought in. The layout was similar to Tiye's with a spacious central sitting area from which various chambers opened. There was a separate bedchamber, four smaller sitting chambers in addition to the large one, and a bathing chamber that was only a little smaller than Tiye's.

Ettu found her way to my new chambers with news the gate guards claimed Tall and Half hadn't left since their shift started. So, either Panouk or the guards were lying, and I knew who I thought most likely. Ettu inspected my new chambers with a practiced eye.

"I wonder what Lady Tiye will think of this?" she asked.

"Maybe she doesn't even know."

"Oh, believe me, my lady, she knows. Word travels fast through the Palace."

"Which chamber do you want?" I asked.

"What do you mean?"

"What am I going to do with so many chambers? I thought

you and Ahmose could each take a chamber for yourself. Maybe Merytre also. And then there's still one to spare."

I considered offering it to Nammu and Belet-ili, but this space already felt like a refuge from the rest of the Palace. I didn't want women I couldn't trust here.

"But those are supposed to be your sitting chambers," Ettu said. "Or you could use one for dressing and perhaps another for storage."

"What do I need five sitting chambers for? This central one is big enough and it's more convenient since it opens onto the hallway. And I only need one chamber to sleep in, yet you are sharing a bedchamber with other women. Strangers. Wouldn't you be more comfortable here?"

"I certainly would, but are you sure?"

"Of course. I will tell Panouk to have extra beds brought in."

Panouk arranged beds for the other four chambers and he seemed quite gracious about it. I had thought he might consider my request too extravagant, but as he told me repeatedly, nothing was too much for Pharaoh's Ornaments. He didn't even blink when I told him I would eat in my chambers at night and to have food sufficient for four people sent to me both then and in the mornings. I would probably still eat in the dining chamber at times, but my companions could eat here rather than going to wherever the servants ate.

The afternoon was half over by the time Ahmose returned. She carried a small sack which she seemed reluctant to let anyone see.

"Did you get everything?" I asked.

"I did," she said. "But it would be best if you don't know too much at this stage. I have a way to get your messages out of the Palace and that's all you need to know."

She retrieved papyrus, a reed pen, and a small pot of ink from her sack. The scholar in me wanted to know everything about her plan. There was knowledge to be gained in the arrangements she was making and I wanted it. But I swallowed down my objection. For now, my main concern needed to be sending a letter to my father and finding out whether Tall and Half were safe. I could get the details from her another time.

Ahmose looked unfazed by my offer of a private chamber, but Merytre greeted the suggestion with wide eyes.

"Me, my lady?" she asked. "You want me to sleep in your chambers?"

"Not in my bedchamber," I said. "You will have a chamber of your own. But since you are the newest of the three women I trust the most, you will select from whatever is left after Ettu and Ahmose have chosen their chambers."

Merytre dropped to her belly on the floor.

"Please," I said to her. "You don't need to do that."

In Babylon, we knelt only for the king. I was accustomed to folk touching their fingers to their lips as a sign of respect, but nobody knelt for me. It made me feel like I was pretending to be of higher status than I was. An imposter.

Merytre rose elegantly to her feet without tripping over her hem like I would have.

"My lady, you have my loyalty," she said.

I had five allies now: Ettu, Ahmose, Tall, Half and Merytre. Assuming I could find Tall and Half, that is. Maybe eventually I would be able to call them all friends, but for now, I was satisfied to know I had people I could trust.

The sun was setting by the time everything was arranged in my new chambers. The escort Panouk had said he would send never came. I wondered whether I should go speak with the gate guards myself anyway, but there hardly seemed any point since they had already told Ettu the men hadn't left.

The four of us passed a cheery evening together, marred only by the lack of news about Tall and Half. A team of servants brought food and we ate in the central sitting chamber. There was roasted duck and whole baked fish. A salad of lettuce, cucumbers and crunchy sweet onions. Three types of bread and two kinds of cheese. Jugs of melon juice and a rich red wine which bore a label claiming it was from Pharaoh's own vineyard.

"Marduk have mercy on me," Ettu said, licking the last of the duck fat off her fingers. "If we eat like this every day, I'm going to be as fat as a pregnant cow."

"I wish we knew Tall and Half were safe," I said.

Ettu winced.

"And here's me, thinking about nothing but my belly," she said.

"They wouldn't expect us not to eat just because we don't know where they are," I said. "But I do wish we could find them. Once I have got a letter out to my father, that needs to be our next priority."

"A letter?" Merytre asked. "My lady, surely you have been told…"

The look on my face must have been sterner than I intended, because she quickly dropped her gaze.

"Of course, it is none of my business," she said.

"Don't be like that," I said. "You are my allies. You should know what we intend."

"We?" Ettu asked.

My gaze shot to Ahmose.

"There is a way to get a letter out of the palace without anyone else knowing," I said. "And here, within the walls of my chambers, we four need to be free to speak our minds and to know we can trust the others. What is shared between us in here must never be told to anyone else. Agreed?"

I looked around our small circle, meeting the eyes of each. Ettu and Merytre both dropped their gaze, as if they were ashamed of something. Ahmose was the only one who held my stare and she looked back at me boldly.

"Ettu?" I asked.

"I have already sworn to serve you, my lady."

"What I ask of you now is more than service. I ask that the four of us become…" I faltered, unsure how to put into words what I wanted from them.

"Family," Merytre said with a faint smile.

I hesitated, wondering whether I had misunderstood the Egyptian word she used. My comfort with the language was improving with each hour, but I still wasn't sure I comprehended all the nuances of what was said, even if I thought I understood the words themselves.

"Yes," I said. "We are all far from our own families. Far from our homes. But none of us is alone. We are together, and together we can be a family. We can make ourselves a new home."

"So you intend to stay?" Ettu asked.

"Of course. What else can I do?"

She shrugged. "I suppose I thought you might find a way to flee. After all, the situation here is clearly not what you expected. I thought you would find a way out and go back to Babylon."

Show Pharaoh what the women of Babylon are made of.

"I cannot," I said. "My father bid me come here. I cannot leave without jeopardising the alliance."

"Even though you were misled as to why you were coming here?" she asked. "I know you expected to be queen. It was what we all expected."

"I can't imagine this is what Father thought he was sending me to, but I am a Princess of Babylon and this is what my king has asked of me. I cannot walk away from my duty, even if the situation is not as I might wish it was."

A half-remember memory teased my brain and I paused to concentrate on it. What was it? Something Tall had said. Queen, he told me. He said it several times and he hadn't sounded happy. Queen.

"Tall knew I wouldn't be queen," I said. "Or he guessed somehow. He was trying to tell me, but I didn't understand."

No, I realised with sudden clarity, *Nammu* knew and he had

overheard her discussing it with Belet-ili. Perhaps they didn't even try to hide it from Tall, since no doubt they both thought him too witless to understand what he heard.

"Nammu," Ettu said, obviously realising the same thing.

"Ishtar knew all along," I said.

"And she told Nammu," she said.

"Nammu told Belet-ili," I said.

That must be the meaning of their sniggers and pointed comments. They knew I wouldn't be queen and were enjoying my misbelief. I should have dismissed them as soon as we arrived.

"You are a stronger woman than I am," Ettu said. "If it was me, I would have left already."

I searched for the right words, not wanting to offend her but feeling like I needed to explain myself more clearly.

"I was raised with an expectation of duty," I said. "I always knew Father would choose my husband for me. That he would choose my fate. I never expected happiness, but I will find a way to be content with what I have."

I looked around at each of them again.

"The only question now is will you join me?"

It was only after Ettu and Merytre went off to their bedchambers that I asked Ahmose when she would prepare her spell.

"Tomorrow morning," she said. "After your letter is ready."

"Not tonight?"

"It must be fresh when it is used. I am not sure how long it will last, but it can be no more than twelve hours. If I prepare it too soon, it will lose its potency before the task is complete."

"Tell me what to expect."

"You must write your letter before the potion is administered. There will be no time to waste once your messenger has drunk it."

"What will happen once it is drunk?" I asked.

"The messenger will take your letter and walk right past the guards unseen."

"The potion will make the messenger invisible?" My tone was sceptical now. I had never heard of such a thing.

"Aah, you don't believe." She wagged her finger at me. "You will see soon enough, my lady. I told you Ahmose would be an invaluable ally."

"Who will take the letter? And how do I ensure it reaches my father?"

"I suppose it must be me," she said. "I will find a courier who can convey it upriver and ensure it makes its way onto a ship heading to Babylon."

"How will you know who to trust? What if you give my letter to someone and they merely throw it away? Or they show it to someone who could cause trouble for me? One of the Palace administrators, or someone who has Pharaoh's ear. How can I be sure my father will receive it?"

"I can get your letter out of the Palace and into the hands of a courier," Ahmose said. "But past that we shall have to trust the gods to ensure it is delivered. I suggest you pray to whichever god you worship. In the meantime, you should have your letter ready by dawn. I will leave as soon as the sun is up."

I spent most of the night turning restlessly in my bed while I mentally composed a letter to Father. It was difficult to find the right words. I needed to alert him to the situation here, but also assure him I would do my duty regardless. I couldn't ignore the fact that perhaps he had known what he sent me to. If that was the case, my writing to complain would serve no purpose other than to disappoint him.

It would be at least a couple of months before I could expect a reply, if he was even inclined to send one, and there was no guarantee his letter would ever reach me. Ships were wrecked in storms, letters went astray, couriers died. All manner of things might occur to prevent his reply from getting to me.

Not that I expected it would change anything. It seemed clear he knew I wouldn't be queen, but did he expect me to be relegated to the status of Ornament and sent to a secondary palace? Regardless of whether the situation I found myself in was what he thought he was sending me to, Father would expect me to do my duty. The alliance must be maintained. At most, he might perhaps send Pharaoh a letter to express his displeasure, but I could hardly expect anything more. But if there was no reply, how would I know my letter reached him?

When the birds began their morning songs shortly before dawn, I rose and went to the little table where I had laid out the writing implements Ahmose procured for me. I dipped the reed pen into the little pot of ink. *To Marduk-apla-idinna*, I wrote.

Father, this letter confirms my safe arrival in Egypt. I am in the city of Thebes, which is a journey of some days downriver from the sea port. On arrival at Thebes, my companions and I were sent to a place called the Palace of the Ornaments, where Pharaoh's many wives live. Pharaoh himself lives elsewhere and I have not yet had opportunity to meet him.

I write to assure you of my continued obedience. I am sure to meet Pharaoh very soon and I will express to him your dedication to the alliance between Babylon and Egypt. I will, as you bid me, always advocate for the benefit of Babylon and be a shining example of a Babylonian woman.

Your dutiful daughter,

Kassaya

I refrained from expressing my disappointment at learning I wouldn't be living in Pharaoh's palace or my dismay that my task of providing Pharaoh with sons would be more difficult than I expected, given there were so many wives to compete for his attention. I had included enough detail for Father to understand the situation, and if it wasn't what he expected for me, it was his decision as to what he did. Either way, I could expect no reply for at least three months, so in the meantime the only thing I could do was get on with establishing myself here.

I read my letter one last time and set it aside to dry. It contained nothing controversial — indeed, perhaps the scribe wouldn't have even bothered to censor it — but I wanted to be certain the letter Father received was exactly as I wrote it.

On the journey to Egypt, I had decided to write to Ishtar, but now the moment had come, resentment filled me and I found myself unwilling to set the reed to the papyrus again. She knew she wouldn't be queen. That was why she had gone to such pains to contrive a way out of it for herself. No, I wouldn't write to her. Not yet, at any rate. I would wait until I could trust myself not to write something bitter.

At the window, I watched the sky fill with orange as the sun rose. It peeked over the distant horizon just as Ahmose came from her bedchamber. Her gaze went straight to the sheet of papyrus on the table.

"It is ready?" she asked.

I nodded. "Are you sure this will work?"

"More or less."

"You aren't certain?" My tone was sharp now.

"One can never be certain, my lady," she said rebukingly. "Even if it is a spell one has used before, one can never be sure the potion is exactly the same. The ingredients might not be as fresh or of the same quality. There might be slightly more or less of one particular item. The air, the temperature, the time of day and month and year. They all affect a spell."

"But if it doesn't work, you will be caught as you leave."

"I will." She looked at me steadily.

"There would be a punishment for trying to smuggle an unauthorised letter out of the Palace. You would be arrested, at the very least."

"I understand. The only question, my lady, is whether you are prepared to take such a risk."

I felt awful for hesitating. I hadn't realised the possibility of discovery would be so high. Was the opportunity to send an uncensored letter to Father worth the risk? Was it fair of me to ask Ahmose to risk her freedom, and perhaps even her life, in such a way?

"I don't know," I said. "Maybe we should think of another plan."

"It would be very valuable to know we can get a messenger

out through the gates," she said. "If I can get out, I can search for Tall and Half."

I wanted to suggest she try leaving without my letter. Then if she was successful, she could go a second time, and if she was caught, there would be no letter for anyone to find. But that put all the risk on her. It would be cowardly of me to suggest such a thing. If Ahmose was prepared to try to get a letter out to my father, I needed to be willing to share the risk.

"Do it," I said. "But find out where Tall and Half are while you are out there. The risk is worth it if we can get news of them as well."

From her sack Ahmose retrieved a clay bottle and an assortment of small linen packets, neatly folded and tied with thread. She laid them out in a row on a table.

"What is in those?" I asked.

"The ingredients for the potion."

"I realise that, but what exactly?"

She shook her head.

"The less you know the better," she said. "At least until we know I can get out. Besides, unless you have the complete recipe and the quantities, the ingredients are of no benefit to you."

"You said you could teach me secret things."

"I can, and I will. But not today."

"I was merely curious."

"Curiosity can be a dangerous thing, my lady."

"I disagree. Knowledge can be dangerous, but curiosity is not. There is much we would never learn if we were not curious."

"That may be," she said. "But it would be best if you know no detail of the potion at this stage."

She opened the little packets and tipped them one by one into the bottle, then replaced the stopper and shook the bottle vigorously.

"It is ready," she said. "Fold your letter and give it to me."

I hesitated once more. Was the risk really worth it?

"Quickly now," she said. "The longer the potion sits undrunk, the more it loses its efficiency."

I folded the letter as she instructed and placed it in her hand. She raised the bottle to her lips and drank, then set the empty vessel on the table.

"You should ensure that is disposed of as soon as I leave," she said. "If I am caught, it would not do to have evidence lying in your chamber."

"How long will the potion take to work?" I asked.

"It works even now. I must go."

"But I can still see you. Something must have gone wrong."

"The potion was not aimed at you, my lady. It only works against whoever I think of as I drink it. I went out to the gates earlier to look at the guards. It is only they who won't see me."

She hurried away without another word. I wished I could follow her, to see whether she made it out of the Palace safely.

"Marduk go with you," I whispered after her. "May Marduk keep you safe."

CHAPTER 27

When Ettu emerged from her bedchamber shortly afterwards, I sent her to dispose of the bottle and the empty packets, and also to listen for any word of Ahmose being caught. While she was gone, I hid the writing implements in a chest.

"Nothing," she said when she returned. "If she was seen, it has been kept quiet."

"I suppose if nobody comes to arrest me, she made it out," I said.

We both jumped as a knock sounded on the door.

"Breakfast, my lady," called a servant.

Ettu hurried to open the door and by then Merytre was also awake. We waited without speaking as servants brought in food and arranged it on the little tables. Merytre poured me a mug of melon juice and it was only when I took it from her that I noticed how my hands shook. I set the mug down before I spilled it. I could only pick at my meal, despite the rich assortment of pastries, breads and cheeses. Both Ettu and Merytre ate heartily. If they were worried for Ahmose, it didn't affect their appetites.

We had barely finished our meal when there came another knock at the door. The three of us exchanged a look and for a moment it seemed we were all frozen. Then Ettu rose and went to answer it.

"Lady Tiye requests the Lady Kassaya attend her in her chambers," a woman's voice said.

Ettu made no reply, only nodded, then closed the door firmly.

"Well," she said. "What do you intend to do this time?"

Tiye seemed like the least of my problems today.

"I suppose my options are to hide in my chambers until she stops summoning me, or go see what she wants," I said.

If nothing else, it would be a welcome distraction from waiting for news about Ahmose.

Yet another knock came and this time my lady's maids poured in. They fussed around me, exclaiming over the unsuitability of the gown I had dressed myself in. I was made to undress, endure being bathed and shaved all over again, even though there surely wasn't a bristle of hair on my entire body. They rubbed me all over with another of the scented oils that made my nose run. At least it softened my skin, which would be important if they continued to insist on shaving me every day.

I listened for any comments from Nammu or Belet-ili, but heard barely a sound from either of them. I caught Belet-ili's eye at one point and she quickly looked away. So, something was brewing with those two.

When one of the maids asked Ettu which wig I wanted to wear, I told her to choose for me, although I quickly regretted it. The hairpiece the maid selected was a short style, with tiny braids that barely came to my chin and which were threaded with bells that tinkled with my slightest movement. The sound was annoying and I already had a headache before she finished fussing with the braids.

After an inordinately long amount of time, they pronounced

me suitably attired. As Ettu shooed the women from my chambers, Nammu approached me.

"My lady," she said. "May I speak with you?"

"What is it?"

"I heard you gave Ettu her own bedchamber, here in your chambers. I wondered which chamber is to be mine."

"I haven't made any such offer to you."

"But I came here with you all the way from Babylon, just as Ettu did. Belet-ili too. Why should Ettu be favoured over us? If she has her own private bedchamber, we should too."

"Ettu has been here with me." I gave Nammu a stern look. "Where have you been? I see you only when the maids come to dress me in the morning and then you disappear."

"I have been assigned sewing work when you don't need me. You never asked me to stay during the day."

Her tone was sullen now. I had been about to tell her I knew she knew I wouldn't be queen, but decided to hold my tongue. I would keep that information for when I needed it.

"I never asked Ettu either," I said instead. "Yet she knew her place was here with me. You and Belet-ili have done the bare minimum required of your position each day and then disappeared. How do I know whether you are really doing other work all day? You could be off wandering the gardens for all I know."

Her cheeks flushed and she gave me a haughty glare.

"It's not fair," she said. "Ettu is no better than me and if she has her own bedchamber, I should have one too."

"Go," I said. "I'm not discussing this further today. If you want to be favoured, you need to work much harder than you have been."

We glared at each other for a few moments and I thought she would continue to argue, but she only turned and strode out. The door slammed behind her.

"Well," Ettu said. "I suppose that was hardly unexpected."

"Did she really think that would convince me to give her a bedchamber?"

"I've never been able to figure out what that girl is thinking. You should be careful, though. Nammu does not like to be rejected."

"Well, I have no further time for her today," I said. "I should go pay Tiye a visit."

Ettu and Merytre accompanied me as far as the hallway that led to Tiye's suite, even though it was a walk of only a few dozen paces.

"Good luck," Ettu said with an expression that could have been either grin or grimace.

When I knocked on Tiye's door, the lady's maid who opened it was not the same one who admitted me yesterday. So it must be true she had lost her position. I felt bad for her, but she had been complicit in locking me in.

Tiye was lounging on one of her many couches, an abandoned piece of needlework beside her. She gave me a haughty glare and as the silence stretched between us, I forced myself to hold my tongue. She had called me here. Let her be the first to speak. She did, at last.

"So," she said. "I find myself slightly impressed. You are not the first to refuse to clean my bathing chamber, but you are the first to find a way out of my suite without doing it. I'm afraid that won't be so easy today."

She gestured towards a window and I finally noticed the shutters were all closed. I assumed they had been nailed shut. I arched my eyebrows at her.

"Surely you realise there are those who will help me," I said. "Even now, they wait out of sight. They will burn your shutters to ash if they must. Think what a mess that would make of your chambers."

She gave me a hard stare, as if trying to assess whether I was bluffing.

"My bathing chamber still needs cleaning," Tiye said.

"That, surely, is your problem."

She didn't look like she would back down. I supposed she couldn't, not if she wanted to keep her position as Top Ornament.

"I have no desire to take your place," I said. "You don't need to try to intimidate me or whatever this is about. Surely we can find a way to live here together in peace."

"You are braver than the average Ornament. Or stupider. I can't quite decide which."

I shrugged. "Call me brave or stupid as you wish, but I have no intention of cleaning your bathing chamber. If you decide to piss all over the floor, your own servants will have to clean it up."

"Every new Ornament cleans my bathing chamber. That is how it has been ever since I arrived sixteen years ago and took the position of Top Ornament from the one who held it at the time."

"How old were you when you came here?"

"Ten years."

So she was twenty-six now. Twelve years older than me. She must surely have borne Pharaoh sons by now. Not only would I not be queen, it seemed any son I had wouldn't be heir. Had Father known this too?

"Too young to be a wife, even to one such as Pharaoh," I said.

"It was an honour and my family was greatly rewarded for it."

"How did you come to be sent here?"

Perhaps if I could get her to tell me her story, she might relax a little. Realise I wasn't the threat she had determined me to be.

"My mother was lady's maid to the queen," she said. "I caught Pharaoh's eye when I was very young. He told her then to save me for him and that he would marry me when I was old enough."

"And he decided you were old enough at ten years? You were but a child."

"Our girls often marry from the age of eleven or twelve. I was not so young."

"You surely didn't arrive here and take the top position at that age."

She made an inelegant noise that sounded rather like a snort.

"Amun, no," she said. "It took me two years. For two long years, I scrubbed the bathing chamber of the woman who was Top Ornament. Dozens of new women arrived after me, but she had taken a particular dislike to me, so I scrubbed her bathing chamber long after I should have handed off that task to someone else."

"What changed?"

"I became a woman, and Pharaoh decided I was very beautiful. Whenever I was alone with him, I spoke to him sweetly and I fulfilled his every desire. When I thought he was ready to hear it, I told him of the poisonous lies his Favourite spread about him."

"Was she really doing such a thing?"

Tiye looked at me steadily.

"Pharaoh believed she was, and Pharaoh's word is truth," she said.

"What happened to her?"

"Pharaoh allows his Ornaments to live in luxury, but in return he expects complete faithfulness and total obedience. He will not suffer a woman being unfaithful in any way."

"She was sent away?"

Was this my way out?

"She was executed." Tiye's expression never changed. If she felt guilt over the woman's death, she hid it well. "Stabbed through the heart. Pharaoh rewarded me with the position of his Favourite and I took her place as Top Ornament. So, you see, Kassaya, I am a dangerous woman to cross."

"I have no desire to take your place," I said earnestly. "I am here because my father sent me to secure the alliance between Babylon and Egypt. This is not what I would have chosen for myself, but I must make the best of it. That doesn't mean I want your position, though. I merely want to live in peace."

"You still have to clean my bathing chamber. In my position, one must be consistent. If I allow you to renege on your duty to me, the Ornaments will think I have lost my edge. They will jostle to replace me and I do not intend to be replaced."

"What if we made an alliance?" I asked. "A treaty of sorts?"

She eyed me and the edges of her lips curled up just the tiniest bit.

"You are refreshing," she said. "If we weren't competitors, I do believe I would quite like you."

"We don't need to be competitors. I have no wish to compete with anyone here."

"Wait until the first time Pharaoh comes to the Palace. Then see the women you thought were your friends turn against you in order to get closer to him."

I understood there would be some measure of jostling for his attention, but why would the women turn on each other?

"What would it take for us to form an alliance?" I asked.

"What do you offer? I have everything I could possibly want. I only have to suggest to Pharaoh there is something I desire and he provides it for me. Jewels, new gowns, furniture, servants. Anything I want is mine. So what can you give me that he cannot?"

"Friendship," I said. "You have all these things and you are surrounded by servants, but are you not lonely? Wouldn't you like to have someone to sit and chat with? Someone who won't spread rumours or gossip about you as soon as you leave the chamber? Someone you can trust to tell you when others lie about you?"

She studied me for a long moment and I knew she would refuse me. What else could I offer? I racked my brain to come up with something that would be of sufficient worth to her.

"I accept," she said, to my surprise.

"I will come to your chambers in the morning as often as I can, to maintain the appearance of cleaning your bathing chamber, which your own servants will need to do. I warn you, though, I won't be able to come every day."

She tipped her head to the side as she studied me.

"You surprise me, Kassaya of Babylon," she said. "I think you may be a woman worth knowing."

CHAPTER 28

*E*ttu and Merytre were in the sitting chamber when I returned. Ettu's new hairstyle indicated her head had finally been shaved, but their flushed faces distracted me before I could comment.

"Is it Ahmose?" I asked.

"You should close the door," Ettu said.

I did and went to sit with them, my heart already pounding an alarm.

"Tell me immediately," I said. "Was she caught?"

"We have heard nothing of her," Ettu said. "There would have been something by now, so I do believe she made it out of the gates."

"What is it then? Have you heard news of Tall and Half? Are they safe?"

"No word of them either, my lady."

"What is it then?"

Ettu nodded to Merytre.

"You tell her," she said. "You are the one who heard the news. I know only what you have told me."

Merytre swallowed and I finally noticed how pale she looked.

My hands trembled and I tucked them between my knees before anyone noticed. Whatever the news was, it must be dire indeed.

"Have you met Lady Nebtu?" Merytre asked.

"She was in the dining chamber yesterday at breakfast." I had met four Ornaments then, but other than the Mitanni — Gilukhipa — the faces of the other three had blurred and I couldn't remember which was Nebtu. "We spoke only briefly."

"She has gone missing," Merytre said.

"Missing?" I repeated.

I waited, but Merytre didn't seem inclined to elaborate.

"Go on," I prodded.

Merytre looked to Ettu, as if asking her to take over the story.

"You may as well tell her," Ettu said. "She will find out sooner or later. Better that she knows as much as possible before…"

Her voice trailed away and a creeping sense of horror filled me. Something was terribly wrong.

"Will someone tell me what has happened?" I asked.

Merytre opened and closed her mouth, but couldn't seem to find any words. At length, Ettu sighed.

"My lady, it seems there is something you should know about this place. Sometimes the women here, they disappear."

"Disappear? How is that possible? There are guards and servants everywhere. A woman cannot even leave the building without being seen, let alone the grounds."

"And yet it happens." Ettu's voice was grim. "Apparently Nebtu is the third woman to disappear this year alone."

"And the fifteenth that I know of," Merytre said. "Fifteen in the years I have worked here."

I looked from one to the other. I might have thought they were joking if it wasn't for the dread on their faces.

"But how?" I asked.

Merytre shook her head. "Nobody knows."

"What are the administrators doing? Panouk and Amankhau. Are they investigating?"

"They pretend to," Merytre said. "But it never seems very exhaustive and their conclusion is always the same: the woman ran away."

"Ran away? From a place where we are guarded at all hours of the day and night?"

"I can tell you only what they say," Merytre said. "And they always say the women have run away."

"What do *you* think?" I asked.

Merytre's eyes widened, as if she hadn't expected to be asked for her opinion.

"There have been rumours," she said slowly.

"What kind of rumours?"

"Men who come in the night and take women away."

"That is ludicrous," I said. "The administrators would never allow such a thing."

Merytre shrugged. "I can only tell you what I have heard."

"But what reason would anyone have to come in and steal away various women?" I asked.

"To return them to their homes?" Ettu suggested. "Rescue groups, if you like, sent by their fathers and brothers after they realise the women here are no better than prisoners."

"Or to sell them into slavery," Merytre said. "Or for dark magic."

"But the administrators are responsible for looking after the residents," I said. "If men are entering the palace, the administrators must have sanctioned it. It would be the grossest breach of their duties if they allowed women to be stolen away. Has nobody reported it to Pharaoh?"

"Not by the likes of me," Merytre said. "I've never even met him."

"But surely one of the Ornaments must have told him," I said. "Send someone to find Panouk. I want to hear from him what is being done to find Nebtu. For the sake of all our safety, we can't allow this to be covered up."

CHAPTER 29

Several hours passed before Panouk came. Ettu had sent three messengers to him by then and I was almost ready to go find the man myself. He bowed and gave me a practised smile. If he was at all aware of how long he had kept me waiting, he gave no sign of it.

"What is being done to look for Nebtu?" I asked.

There seemed no point in hedging around what I wanted to know. He surely already knew of her disappearance and there was no way to ask without making it clear that I also knew.

"My lady, all possible efforts are being made to locate her." Panouk's tone dripped with obsequiousness. "However, after due investigation, it seems likely she has returned to her father's household."

"Has that been verified with her father?" I asked.

"Hmm?" Panouk gave me a blank look, as if he didn't quite hear my question.

I repeated it, although I was sure he had heard me and was merely stalling while he thought of a reply.

"Oh, yes, of course," he said. "A messenger will be sent to confirm her safe arrival."

"I'd like to speak with the messenger," I said. "The one who hears her father say she has returned there."

"That won't be necessary," Panouk said. "I will be sure to send word to you once we have confirmation. My lady, I wasn't aware you and Lady Nebtu had grown so close in such a short time."

"I will expect the messenger to be sent to my chambers as soon as they have reported to you."

He spluttered.

"Really, my lady—"

"Did you not say you were here to fulfil my every wish?" I asked.

"Of course, my lady, but—"

"It is my wish to speak to the messenger who brings Nebtu's father's confirmation. Is this not something that is in your power to arrange? I thought you controlled everything within the Palace."

"Of course, my lady. I will ensure the messenger is sent to you."

It seemed that appealing to Panouk's pride in how he ran the Palace could be a useful way to manage him.

The day passed slowly as we waited for news of Ahmose, Tall and Half, and Nebtu. By sunset I couldn't stand it any longer. I had spent the last couple of hours pacing the sitting room and by now I knew the mosaic pattern on the floor well enough to have drawn it. Ettu and Merytre perched on couches and although they were comfortable enough to sleep on, neither looked at ease.

"I am going to speak with the gate guards," I said at last.

"Are you sure that is wise?" Ettu asked. "If Ahmose was caught, it would be better if you seem to know nothing about it. If you go asking after her, it proves you knew she was trying to get out, and it would be logical to assume you sent her. You could be arrested yourself."

"Or worse." Merytre's tone was filled with foreboding.

"Surely not," I said, although I didn't feel as secure in my safety as I might have a day or so ago. Not after knowing there was a possibility that men had taken Nebtu from the Palace. From right under the administrator's noses. Perhaps even with their knowledge since there seemed to be so little attempt at any investigation.

"Wait a little longer," Ettu urged. "Come sit beside me. She will be back soon and you might well ruin the spell if you go asking after her."

She patted the couch, which was indeed big enough for two. I sat, although my feet were still restless and I tapped my thighs.

"Besides, what do you hope to achieve?" Merytre added. "If nobody saw her leave, asking the guards won't give you any information."

"But if the spell went wrong and they *did* see her, I might be able to tell," I said. "Surely their faces or their body language will give them away, even if they lie to me."

"It is too risky," Ettu said. "If she was caught and you go asking after her, you risk exposing yourself. And if she wasn't caught, you might reveal her absence and make it that much harder for her to get back in."

"Not if I say I haven't seen her all day and wondered if someone can tell me whether she left the grounds," I said.

"The day guards will be off duty by now," Merytre said. "And if anyone saw her, it would have been them."

"Just wait," Ettu said. "No good can come of you going to the gates."

I sighed and sank back against the couch. They were right. I hated waiting and not knowing. It made me feel awful to think Ahmose might be in trouble while I lazed around, but it was true I risked not only my own freedom, but hers as well.

I jumped when someone knocked on the door. Merytre rose to answer it and my heart pounded as I waited to find out who it was. It couldn't be Ahmose herself. Surely she wouldn't knock and wait to be admitted. Perhaps it was one of the administrators, come to say Ahmose had been arrested and to question me as to what I knew about my tutor's attempt to leave the Palace compound.

But it was only the servants with our evening meal. Savoury aromas reached my nose as they laid out platters on various tables, then hurried out. Merytre closed the door behind them.

"Well," Ettu said. "I hardly feel like I could eat right now."

"I certainly cannot," I said.

I glanced at Merytre at just the right moment to catch the indecision that flashed across her face.

"Go ahead," I said to her. "If you are hungry, you should eat. Marduk knows they brought plenty of food. There is no point it going to waste."

Merytre didn't hesitate any longer. Maybe there had been times in her life when meals were not regular. I myself had never known anything but the confidence that food would be available at any time I wanted it. I must remember that some of my companions mightn't have had that certainty.

We sat up long into the night. I tried to restrain my urge to pace the chambers, sensing it was becoming irritating to Ettu and Merytre. Not that either of them would have commented. In Babylon, it was not a servant's place to object to her mistress's actions and I doubted it was any different here. Both women were yawning and my head swam with weariness, although I was sure I wouldn't be able to sleep.

"Go to bed," I said at last. "There is no point in all of us waiting up."

"Do you intend to sleep yourself?" Ettu asked.

"I will sit up a while longer. I want to know immediately if Ahmose returns."

"Then I will sit with you," she said.

"Me too," Merytre added.

As the hours passed, my eyes drooped and I leaned my head against the back of the couch. It wouldn't matter if I closed my eyes. It wasn't like I would fall asleep. I would just sit here with my eyes closed and listen for Ahmose's return.

J woke to the sound of footsteps in the hallway. For a moment, I was disorientated at finding myself lying on a couch. Sunlight glinted around the edges of the closed shutters. Ettu and Merytre were each curled in a chair. Ettu had her feet tucked under her skirt as if they had gotten cold overnight, and Merytre rested her cheek on her hands. They stirred and blinked sleepily. The door opened.

"Ahmose!" Relief filled me, so sudden I almost cried. "Where in Marduk's name have you been?"

"Sorry, my lady." Ahmose closed the door and sagged against it. Her eyes were large in a too pale face. "I had a small problem."

Ettu jumped up to help her over to a chair.

"Sit," she said. "I will bring you some wine."

"There is food left from last night." Merytre got up more slowly, rubbing her eyes as if she couldn't quite wake up. "I will get you something. You must be starved."

Ahmose gulped down the wine and accepted a plate of food, but set it on her lap.

"I should explain," she said.

"No, eat first," I said, although I didn't want to wait to hear her news. "You must be starved."

Ahmose didn't demur any longer, but gobbled down the bread and cheese. Merytre fetched her some more and she ate the second piece more slowly. At last, she wiped her mouth and sighed.

"I cannot remember the last time I was so hungry," she said. "I do apologise for my rudeness."

"Nonsense," I said. "You were gone for more than a day. Did you have nothing to eat or drink in that time?"

"Not at all," she said.

"Well, go on," Ettu said. "Tell us what happened."

"Did you get my letter to a courier?" I asked.

Ahmose nodded.

"I did. The spell worked perfectly to get me out. I waited until the guards opened the gates to admit someone and I simply strolled right through. They never saw me. I went to the docks and was able to find a captain who is heading up the Great River in a day or two. He agreed to take your letter and see it onto a ship bound for Babylon."

I sighed with relief. Father would at least know of the circumstances here, assuming the letter reached him. There was no guarantee it would, but the first hurdle — and possibly the greatest — had been passed. We now knew we could get an uncensored letter out of the Palace.

"Did you hear any news of Half and Tall?" Ettu asked.

My relief turned to embarrassment that I had been thinking only of myself. Our two companions were still out there somewhere, or at least, I hoped they were.

"It took so long to deal with the letter, there wasn't much time to ask around," Ahmose said. "If they made it out of the Palace grounds, they should be quite a distinctive pair, but nobody at the docks had seen them. There was no time to go anywhere else as the sun was setting and I wasn't sure how much longer the spell would last. Most folk had left by then anyway."

"So people at the docks could see you, but not the guards?" Merytre asked.

"The spell was directed at the guards," Ahmose said. "Of course everyone else could see me."

"Oh." Merytre looked as puzzled as I felt.

I didn't understand how it could be possible for one person to see Ahmose while she was invisible to another. I burned to learn her magic.

"When I approached the gates on my return, I could tell the guards had seen me," Ahmose continued.

"Oh no," Ettu breathed.

"What did you do?" I asked.

"I turned back," she said. "There was no point trying to get inside if the spell had worn off. If they recognised me, they would want to know why there was no record of me having left the grounds, or indeed of approval for such a thing. And if they didn't recognise me, what was I to do? Claim to be an inhabitant of the Palace and hope they believed me without checking with one of the administrators?"

"The administrators would surely have recognised you," I said. "Or Amankhau would, at least."

"What happened then?" Merytre asked.

"I found myself a sheltered spot to spend the night," Ahmose said. "I couldn't think of what else to do. I was waiting at the markets before dawn, ready to find the items I needed to replenish the spell."

"How did you pay for them?" Ettu asked.

Ahmose gave her a small shrug.

"I stole what I could and used such payment as a woman has available to her when I couldn't," she said.

I wasn't sure I understood, but both Ettu and Merytre nodded, and I didn't want to look foolish by asking.

"Then I had to wait until the guards had reason to open the gates."

"And they never saw you?" Ettu asked.

"No," Ahmose said. "Although at one point my sandal scraped on the path and I was sure I would be caught. One of the guards heard me and they both started looking around. A spell such as this only works as long as nobody is looking too hard. I couldn't decide whether to stand still and hope they didn't see me, or to run."

"Which did you choose?" I asked.

"I ran." She gave me a tight smile. "I thought if I stood there and they saw me, I would be arrested. So I raced in while the gates were open and hid in the gardens. I was close enough to hear them arguing about it afterwards. They both believed something had gotten inside, but couldn't agree on what. One of them thought they should report it to Panouk and the other spoke of hares and cats. In the end, they agreed it must have been just an animal and it wasn't necessary to report it."

"Thank Marduk they didn't," I said. "There would have been guards searching every cubit of the grounds if they reported that something came inside."

"They would have found me had they looked hard enough," Ahmose said. "I don't believe they are very good guards and it would be worth remembering the day guards are more worried about saving themselves than reporting a possible unauthorised entry. I hid where I was, in the middle of some thick bushes, and waited until the guards were busy with something else before I made my way through the grounds."

She yawned then, an eye watering yawn that reminded me she was an old woman.

"Go to bed," I said. "Sleep for as long as you need. Once you are rested, we will discuss our next move. We need to focus on finding Tall and Half now."

CHAPTER 31

*I*t had been a couple of days since I last ate in the dining chamber, so I decided to go for breakfast. It would give me a chance to find out whether there was any word on Nebtu and I might also be able to ask when I'd meet Pharaoh. It seemed strange I'd been here for several days now and he hadn't asked for me.

By the time my lady's maids arrived to dress me, servants had also brought food. I noticed a couple of the maids looking curiously at the tables laden with breads, cheeses, fruit and gruel. Likely they were wondering how I ate so much by myself. My stomach was growling by the time they left. Neither Nammu nor Belet-ili said a word in all that time, and I never even caught their eyes.

"I will come with you," Ettu said.

"Stay here and eat. I'm sure I can remember the way to the dining chamber."

"It is not appropriate for you to be seen wandering the Palace alone," she said.

"Most Ornaments take several lady's maids everywhere they

go," Merytre said, casting a longing look at the food. "We should both go with you."

"I will be fine on my own," I said. "Besides, the gruel will be cold by the time I return. Come and find me after you have eaten if you must, but I will go by myself."

I hurried out before they could argue any further and found the dining chamber with only a couple of wrong turns. There were more than a dozen women there this morning and easily double that number of lady's maids lined up along the wall. I scanned the faces of the Ornaments and recognised only Henutmire. She nodded at me. I decided to call that an invitation and settled myself at the table beside hers. Before I could speak, servants were already offering me their trays.

"Good morning," I said to Henutmire once the servants were finally satisfied I had enough food on my table.

She gave me a small smile. Her face was pale and her mouth tight. From what I could see, she didn't seem to have touched any of the food on her table, although she sipped occasionally from a mug.

"Is there any news?" Might as well get straight to the point.

"Of Nebtu? Nothing." Henutmire sighed and shook her head. "The administrators say she snuck out and returned to her father's house."

"You don't believe that?"

She glanced around as if checking whether anyone else was within hearing distance. A servant woman slowly made her way between the tables with a jug and Henutmire waited until she left before she leaned over to whisper to me.

"I don't believe it for a moment," she said. "This happens every few months. An Ornament disappears, or sometimes a lady's maid, and the official story is always that they left. Sometimes we are told they returned to their family. Other times they say the woman had a secret lover and ran off with him. But it is always the same. A woman who disappears in the middle of the night and is never heard from again."

"Is there anyone here Nebtu might send a message to? Someone she is close to?"

"Me." Henutmire gave me a look that seemed heavy with significance. "She and I arrived in the same week and we are as close as it is possible for two women to be in this place. I would know if she had some secret lover, or if she was planning to run away. She wouldn't leave without telling me."

I ate almost without noticing and tasted none of it. Where was Nebtu and what had happened to her? Had she angered Pharaoh and been sent from the Palace in disgrace in the dead of night? Or had something more sinister happened? I didn't know what to think.

Were other women in danger? My companions and I were probably safe enough, at least while we were in my chambers. The door could be barred from the inside and it would be hard for anyone to remove one of us during the night without the others noticing. But I was the only Ornament I knew of who shared her chambers with her maids. Maybe Ettu was right about not wandering the hallways alone.

I didn't want to risk disturbing Ahmose while she rested, so I decided to go out to the gardens. I hadn't had a chance to explore them yet, and surely I would be perfectly safe outside during the day. The grounds were constantly patrolled and surely a woman couldn't disappear in broad daylight and in view of the guards.

As I emerged from the Palace, it was like a great weight rolled off my shoulders. The sun was midway to its peak, blazing from an endless blue sky. A lone bird circled high overhead. The grounds were immaculately maintained, with beds full of carefully planted flowers interspersed with stands of palm trees. A wooden bench beneath an acacia tree provided a pleasant place to sit and take in the view. Bees buzzed, a bird chirped from a leafy branch, and the fragrance of blooming flowers assaulted my nose.

I wandered without any destination, just following one of the paths winding through the grounds. This was the first time I had really taken in the size of the Palace. I had thought Father's stronghold was large, but this place was truly enormous. I supposed it had to be to accommodate several hundred Ornaments, plus the many servants needed to maintain both the women and their home. Amankhau had said there were several thousand people living here.

The reminder that I was just one of Pharaoh's many wives hit me all over again, but when I examined my feelings, I realised I had grown somewhat accustomed to the idea, despite how shocking it was to start with. I never wanted to be a queen anyway. It was Ishtar who was raised to expect such a thing. Not me.

I would be happier being out of the public view and perhaps a life in the Palace of the Ornaments wouldn't be so bad. Without the pressures of ruling a country, I might still have time for learning. There was far more that Ahmose could teach me and she surely wasn't the only learned woman in this place. All I had ever wanted was to spend my life learning. Maybe I could be happy here.

 wandered through the grounds until the sun reached its peak. By then, the air was so hot, my lungs burned with every breath. The tall walls blocked any breeze and I realised what a luxury it was that my chambers were up so high. Those whose chambers were on the ground level — like my original chamber — must suffer terribly on hot days.

To my surprise, I saw nobody while I was out walking, not even a guard, although at times I felt like someone watched me. Perhaps they hid themselves away to give an illusion of privacy to those who used the grounds. I found a pretty little pond positioned beneath shady trees and sat there for a while, watching a pair of ducks drift lazily across the surface. I envied how cool they must feel with their legs in the water. Eventually the heat and my thirst drove me back inside.

I opened the door to my chambers as quietly as I could, silently thanking whoever had ensured the hinges were well oiled, and slipped in to find all three women in the sitting chamber.

"I thought you would still be sleeping," I said to Ahmose.

"I slept long enough," she said. "Someone needs to go back out to search for Tall and Half."

"I think I should go," Ettu said. "Merytre and I have discussed it. We think that Ahmose, being older, should continue to rest and one of us should go. Since Merytre doesn't know Tall and Half, we agree it should be me."

"I could go," I said.

"No, my lady," Merytre said quickly. "Someone is more likely to come looking for you than for the likes of us."

"Nobody will notice an absent lady's maid," Ettu added, "and if they do, you only have to say you sent me on an errand. Fetching something for you, or finding something. That wouldn't be so much of a lie."

"But where will you go?" I asked. "You don't know anyone out there and you have no idea where they might have gone."

"Neither do you," Ettu said. "But someone needs to look for them."

"It should be me," Ahmose said. "It is my spell and I should take the risk."

"No," I said. "I agree you should rest."

She was too old to be tramping around the city all night, although I didn't think she would react well if I said that. Ahmose looked as if she wanted to argue, but she only touched her fingers to her lips.

"As you wish, my lady," she said.

Ettu and I eyed each other.

"I will go," she said. "They will miss you long before they miss me."

"Very well then," I said, although I wanted to argue.

We agreed she would wait until dark so she had more cover to hide in and when the sun sank low over the horizon, Ahmose slipped away to her chamber to prepare the potion. I longed to watch but figured she would bring the ingredients out to the sitting chamber if she wanted anyone to see. She returned with a small bottle, which she offered to Ettu.

Ettu removed the stopper and sniffed the contents. She screwed up her nose and quickly replaced the stopper. I caught only the faint scent of an odour I didn't recognise. It didn't smell particularly offensive to me, but then, I wasn't the one who would have to consume it.

"Take it with you," Ahmose said. "Once you have seen the faces of the guards, drink it all, then hide the bottle. As best I can figure, this will shield you for about twelve hours. So you must be back before dawn and, mind, the guards at the gate must be the same ones you saw before you drank it. The potion will not work against new faces."

"What do we do if she cannot return in time?" I asked.

"Then I will have to go in search of her," Ahmose said.

"We should choose a place to meet," Ettu said. "There is no point me wandering around aimlessly because I can't get past the guards while you search for me."

They agreed on a spot just a block or two away, marked by a shady tree. Ahmose said it was well out of sight of the men stationed at the front gates.

"Does it work immediately?" Ettu asked, eyeing the bottle in her hand.

"It should, but wait a few moments after you have drunk it before you try to leave. That will be long enough."

"How will I know, though? What if I get there and they can see me?"

"You could say I have sent you to ask if there have been any visitors for me," I said. "It is no secret I am concerned about Tall and Half. Tell the guards I sent you to enquire whether they have come asking for me."

"That's a good idea." Ettu's face looked a little less tense now. "Well, I suppose I should leave."

"Go," Ahmose said. "Remember you have twelve hours at most."

"Good luck," I said. "And be careful."

"I will," Ettu said. "I will return before dawn."

CHAPTER 33

I spent the night on one of the couches in the sitting room, a lamp burning low on a table beside me. Ahmose went off to her chamber and Merytre offered to sit with me, but I sent her to bed too. Although I tried to sleep, I was too worried about Ettu to do more than doze.

The chamber was still dark when the doorknob rattled. I was awake and sitting up even as the door swung open. My heart pounded in anticipation. Ettu slipped inside and closed the door behind her. She didn't look surprised to see me waiting.

"I have news of them," she said without preamble. "And they are safe as far as I can tell."

"Did you speak with them? Come, sit down. You look exhausted. I will fetch you a drink."

Ettu's face was pale with dark shadows beneath her eyes. She sank onto a couch and accepted a mug of melon juice with a nod of thanks. I waited while she drank, biting my lip to stop myself from questioning her.

"They are in Pharaoh's palace," she said once she had quenched her thirst.

"Are you sure?" I was so surprised, I hardly knew what to ask.

176

"I have not spoken with them. But I found a well and spent the early part of the evening there, asking anyone who came to get water whether they knew of them. There was a woman who works as a kitchen servant in Pharaoh's palace. She told me of two men who arrived recently. She described them as a little man and an idiot."

I sighed. I knew it was unlikely that folk here would be any more accepting than those at home, but I had thought I would be able to shield them. Without being queen, I had little power to protect them, especially if they were not here with me.

"Apparently they went to the palace and asked if Pharaoh was in need of entertainers," Ettu said.

While we were on the ship, Half had asked Ahmose whether there were dwarfs in Egypt and she told us of a woman who worked as an entertainer. That must have been what gave them the idea.

"Are you certain it was Tall and Half?" I asked.

"There is surely no other pair of men in Thebes who could be mistaken for them. Apparently Pharaoh found Half's appearance comical and he was delighted with the way Tall speaks and how he flaps his hands. He has allowed them to stay in his palace and will provide them with food and beds for as long as they continue to amuse him."

"And what happens to them once he no longer finds them amusing?" I asked.

"I didn't dare to ask. I hope they would merely be turned out, not..."

Her voice trailed away and I knew she was thinking the same as I was. The people here seemed cruel and indifferent to the value of a human life. Would Tall and Half be executed once they no longer amused Pharaoh?

"It was clever of them, really, to secure positions within Pharaoh's palace," Ettu said. "They could be very useful for you."

"We need to get a message to them."

"I am sure they are working on the same thing. If we can establish a channel of communication with them, you would be the first to know of any news."

"Such as when Pharaoh plans to visit the Ornaments?" I suggested, remembering again I hadn't yet met my "husband" and there had been no word of when that would occur. I had meant to ask at breakfast, but had forgotten by the time Henutmire told me what she knew about Nebtu.

"I am sure there will be much of value to learn if we had a way of communicating with them," Ettu said.

"I am pleased to know they are safe," I said. "I had feared a worse fate for them."

"Me too."

She didn't comment further, but the light blush to her cheeks reminded me of seeing her and Half together as we sailed. I wanted to ask whether something more than a friendship had developed between them, but couldn't think of how to do so without sounding nosy.

"You should go to bed," I said instead. "You must be exhausted."

"I did walk quite a long way," she said. "I'm only sorry I couldn't make direct contact with them."

"But now we know they are safe and where they are. That is far more than we had before."

Ettu went off to bed. A great yawn took me by surprise and I suddenly found myself too weary to get up. The couch was soft and I sank back into it. As I drifted off to sleep, I wondered whether Tall and Half were comfortable in Pharaoh's palace. Did they have proper beds, or did they sleep on the floor or a pile of hay in the stables? I fell asleep before I could spend any more time worrying about their accommodation.

Over breakfast the next morning, we discussed how we might make contact with the men.

"Could you send a message through the Palace scribe?" Ettu

asked. "Given they are your own companions who travelled with you from Babylon, surely that would be authorised."

"But any reply would come back to the scribe first," Merytre said. She darted a glance at me as if still unsure whether it was permissible for her to speak her mind. "They might reply with information we wouldn't want him to see."

"That could cause a lot of trouble for me," I said.

"What if I took the potion again and tried to get to them?" Ettu suggested. "Ahmose, could you get me past the guards of Pharaoh's palace?"

But Ahmose shook her head.

"I don't know what they look like," she said. "And neither do you. Even if you knew their faces, I don't know whether I could make one potion work against both sets of guards."

I sank back against the couch, feeling defeated. We had to find a way to get a message to them.

"But I could go myself." Ahmose spoke slowly, as if she was still sorting through her thoughts. "If I take enough ingredients with me, I could make a second potion once I have seen Pharaoh's guards. Then I could locate our men, and find out what they have learned. I don't know whether the second potion would cancel out the first one so I might need to make another to get past the guards here when I return. I might also have to wait until the other potions wear off before I try to get back."

"It sounds terribly complicated," Ettu said with a frown.

"It is a lot to ask of you," I said. "And you still look tired. I think we should wait at least another day or two first."

"Better to move while we know where they are," Ahmose replied. "What if we delay and then discover they have already left Pharaoh's palace, or been turned out?"

"I agree," Ettu said. "I think we need to make contact as soon as possible. What if they try to send you a message in the meantime? They might not know any messages will be read by someone else."

"Maybe they already have," I said. "They might have sent messages that contain information we wouldn't want anyone else to know."

"Like what?" Ettu asked. "They don't know we know where they are or that we are using illicit means to try to get to them."

"But they might have heard things about the Palace of the Ornaments and try to warn me," I said. Like the fact that women went missing from here. "Even if such messages are not delivered to me, it creates suspicion. The scribe would surely report such a thing and the administrators might already be watching for any sign that I'm breaking the rules."

"Then we must act quickly," Ahmose said decidedly. "I will go tonight."

CHAPTER 34

*I*t seemed best for Ahmose to wait for the cover of darkness so there was less risk of anyone else spotting her. In the meantime, we all agreed I needed to act like any other woman trying to settle into a new home. Rather than confining myself to my chambers with my lady's maids and my tutor, I needed to be seen.

I decided to start with a walk around the grounds. Merytre accompanied me, while Ettu stayed with Ahmose. With Nebtu's disappearance, it seemed wise for nobody to be alone.

Inside the Palace, the air was relatively cool, so the heat outside took me by surprise. Even though it was only midmorning, the day was already hot.

"What season is this?" I asked Merytre as we made our way along a path.

"*Shemu*, my lady, but it is late. The harvests should be almost finished and soon the season turns to *akhet.*"

"Is that when the floodwaters recede?" Ahmose had told us about the seasons, but I couldn't remember which was which.

"*Akhet* is when the water rises up over the land."

"Of course, the inundation. I remember now."

"If you think it is hot today, wait until *akhet* starts," she said. "After that comes *peret*, when the waters recede. That is the most pleasant time of year and the days will be much cooler."

It was summer when we left Babylon, with clear skies and hot days. As summer ended, the rainy season would begin, when nearly all the year's rain would fall. That would be somewhere around *peret* as the people here measured the seasons, as best I could tell. It still seemed strange to me that this country had no rainy season.

Merytre cleared her throat, drawing me from my musing, and I finally noticed Sutem, the guard who helped me escape from Tiye's chambers on my first day here. He had stopped a little in front of us on the path and the slight curve of his lips suggested amusement.

"Good morning," I said to him.

He bowed, his gaze flicking between Merytre and me.

"This is my lady's maid, Merytre," I said.

"Oh, you don't need to introduce me, my lady," she said quickly.

"Do you already know each other?" I asked.

"Well, we haven't actually met before," she stammered.

"I already knew your name," Sutem said to her. "You have lived in the Palace for longer than I have worked here, but I know most of the residents. You don't come out much."

"No, usually my mistresses have kept me well occupied indoors." Merytre seemed to have regained her composure now. "But my lady here is…" Her voice trailed away.

"Different?" Sutem suggested with a grin.

Merytre only nodded.

Folk had always viewed me as different. Odd. Unusual. All things I had heard muttered about me in my father's palace. Maybe that was why I was drawn to people like Tall and Half. I, too, was an outsider, although my life was far easier than theirs. I tried to find a response that wouldn't sound defensive, but Sutem spoke first.

"Were you intending to walk around the gardens?" he asked.

"Yes." Relief filled me at the change of topic. "We thought some fresh air would be…"

"Refreshing?" he suggested with another grin.

"Yes." I couldn't help but smile back.

"Have you seen the pleasure lake yet?"

"No. Perhaps you could direct us to it?"

"Let me show you."

He stepped off the path and gestured for us to pass him, then fell in behind us.

We followed the path as it wound through the gardens and around the side of the Palace. It was a much longer walk than I anticipated and sweat dripped down the back of my neck. My sandals rubbed at the raw spots that hadn't quite healed yet. I was rather sorry I had agreed long before we got there.

But at last we emerged around a corner and the lake lay ahead of us. It was far bigger than I expected. I supposed what I had pictured would have more properly been described as a pond, like the one I had already found. This was a vast expanse of water that stretched as far as I could see. Papyrus grew around the edges and pink lotus floated on its surface. A breeze wafted over us, no doubt cooled by its passage over the lake.

"It is enormous," I said.

"Pharaoh's Favourite told him she wanted a pleasure lake," Sutem said. "So he had one made for her."

The woman who was Favourite before Tiye perhaps? Surely if it was Pharaoh's current Favourite, Sutem would have named her.

"You mean someone dug a hole that big?" I asked. "And then brought water to fill it?"

"A whole lot of someones, I would think," Sutem said.

"Goodness." The lake seemed even more impressive now. I

spotted a wooden boat, much like the ones we had sailed to Thebes on, drawn up on the shore. "Does anyone sail here?"

"Sometimes," Sutem said.

"Have you ever sailed on the lake, Merytre?" I asked.

"Me? Oh, no, my lady. Sailing the pleasure lake is not for the likes of me."

"We should do it some time," I said. "I have sailed on the Purattu River many times, but never on a lake like this."

We used to swim in the Purattu, too, on hot days.

"Does anyone swim in it?" I asked.

Sutem laughed, although he quickly tried to cover it with a cough.

"Why is that funny?" I asked.

"Because most of the women who live here would not want to be seen in such a state of disarray," he said.

"I would think the opportunity to cool down on a hot day would be worth a few moments of disarray," I said, a little stiffly.

"Me too," Sutem said. "But apparently you and I are in the minority here."

"What about you, Merytre?" I asked. "Would you swim in the lake?"

"Oh, no, my lady," she said. "I don't know how to swim."

"Well, you wouldn't have to *actually* swim," I said. "You could wade in the shallows, or sit in the water. It would be lovely on a hot day."

But Merytre blushed and studied the ground. Wondering what Sutem had made of her response, I shot him a glance and found he, too, looked rather red. Had I said something wrong? I'd have to ask Merytre later in private. I had obviously embarrassed them both.

"Perhaps we should go back inside," I said. "It is very hot and we have been out here for quite a long time."

Merytre was quick to agree.

"The nearest entrance is just over there." Sutem pointed. "Head towards those dom palms and you'll see it."

"Thank you for showing us the lake," I said. "I hope we didn't keep you from your duties."

"Not at all," he said with an easy grin that seemed to include both Merytre and me. "It was a pleasure."

CHAPTER 35

The guards at the door admitted us without question, although I was sure I'd never seen either of them before. The hallway we entered had walls painted with disturbing images of creatures that seemed half human and half animal. I tried not to look at them as we passed.

"I'm sorry if I embarrassed you out there," I said.

"You don't need to apologise to me," Merytre said.

"But I do. I obviously said the wrong thing, although I'm not sure what."

I waited, hoping she might volunteer some information.

"Will you tell me what I did?" I asked when she didn't reply. "I truly didn't mean to embarrass you, but if I don't know what I did, I will likely do it again without realising."

Merytre still didn't reply except to sigh.

"Please," I said.

"It's Sutem," she said finally.

"Yes, I know. He was the one who helped me down from Tiye's window."

"No, I mean I was embarrassed about Sutem. I've never spoken to him before."

I shot her a look to find her blushing furiously and finally understood.

"Oh, you have a crush on him," I said.

"No," she said quickly. "I just… find him attractive."

"So why haven't you spoken to him until now?"

"Because he is not permitted inside the Palace and I have little reason to venture outside."

"Well, perhaps I could send you on some errands out to the gardens," I said. "I might suddenly have a desire for, oh I don't know, some freshly picked flowers or something."

"Please don't," she said. "It would be too embarrassing. I could feel my cheeks go red as soon as he looked at me. He probably thinks me the biggest fool by now."

I, of all people, could sympathise with her blushing. My cheeks went bright red for the slightest reason.

"Actually, I think he was sneaking just as many looks at you as you were at him," I said.

"Really?" She eyed me as if wondering whether I was joking, or maybe lying.

"Of course. Surely you noticed."

Perhaps if I could give her a little confidence, she might find the courage to speak to him. Although Marduk knew I was the last person who knew anything about talking to men. Look how I stumbled over that conversation with Khaemmalu the other night. My cheeks heated at the memory.

"Why are you blushing?" Merytre asked. "If you don't mind me asking, my lady."

I stammered, suddenly unable to string any words together.

"But of course, it is none of my business," she said. "You don't need to explain yourself to the likes of me."

"I don't mind telling you. I just… couldn't figure out how."

"You were thinking about a man, weren't you? Oh, do tell. I swear to Amun I won't tell anyone else."

"I was thinking about someone I met the night we arrived."

I told her about my conversation with Khaemmalu and my embarrassment at how he must have thought I was flirting with him.

"I know his name, but have never met him," Merytre said. "He only works the night shift and I have never had a reason to leave the building at night."

"He is very handsome, which makes it even more embarrassing," I confessed. "He probably has women flirting with him all the time and I am mortified he thinks I was too."

"Maybe he doesn't. Or maybe he hopes you were."

"Marduk, I don't know which would be worse."

Merytre's laughter echoed down the empty hallway.

We slipped into my chambers quietly so as not to disturb Ahmose if she was still sleeping, only to find her and Ettu waiting in the sitting chamber, their faces tight.

"Has something happened?" I asked.

"I was going through your clothing chests," Ettu said. "Looking for anything that needs to be adjusted. The Palace has a team of sewers and I've scheduled them to work on your wardrobe. When I pulled out that golden tunic you were wearing when we arrived, this fell out."

She held out her hand to show me a finger ring. I took it from her for a closer look. Even I could tell it was a very fine piece. The largest red sapphire I had ever seen set in a delicate silver band carved with a trailing pattern of lotus leaves.

"It's beautiful," I said, offering it back to her.

"Have you ever seen it before?" she asked.

"No, but I know there are whole chests of jewels somewhere. It must have gotten mixed up with my clothes."

I didn't know how that might have happened since I hadn't ever worn this particular finger ring, but it seemed like the most obvious explanation.

"It's not yours," Ettu said. "Ishtar chose every item in those chests herself and Nammu, Belet-ili and I had to sit through many, many sessions where she viewed trays of jewels and made her selections. This piece is one I have never seen before."

I frowned at her.

"So where did it come from then?" I asked. "It must have been in one of those chests."

"Something else happened today," she said. "Apparently one of Lady Tiye's favourite finger rings has gone missing from her chambers. A ruby sapphire in a silver setting."

My gaze locked onto the ring in her hand.

"What are you saying?" I asked. "Do you think that is Tiye's?"

"I do." Her tone was grim. "And I think someone planted it in your chest."

"But why?" I asked. "Even if someone is trying to make it look like I stole it from her, what reason would Tiye have to go through my clothing chests to find it? She has no access to my chambers and there is almost always one of us here. Surely there is no point planting a stolen item in a place it will never be found."

Ettu only shrugged.

"I don't know, my lady," she said. "But I think you should be very careful. Lady Tiye's finger ring didn't accidentally fall into your chest."

"Did you say it was the golden tunic you found it in? I thought you sent it to be cleaned?"

"I did, and I took receipt of it myself when it was returned. I was the one who put it away in that chest. There was no finger ring wrapped in it at that time. Someone has put it there since then."

"But who would do such a thing?" I asked.

"Exactly," she said.

There was a brief knock on the door and Ettu's hand closed over the finger ring. My army of lady's maids swept in, led by Nammu. They all prostrated themselves on the floor.

"Good afternoon, my lady," Nammu said after I bid them to

rise. It was the first time she had spoken to me since our discussion about her not being offered a bedchamber in my suite and I was surprised at how cheery she sounded. "We heard Ettu has arranged for alterations to be made to your wardrobe so we have come to collect the items that need to go to the sewers."

I shot a glance at Ettu and found her frowning. Had she not expected Nammu to collect the gowns just yet?

"Go ahead," I said. "As long as you don't need me to try on anything today."

"Oh no," Nammu assured me. "I have a very good eye for sizing. I can pick what will need to be adjusted, although I expect it will be almost everything. Your sister is a little more generous in the bust than you are and her skirts are almost indecently short on you."

I was only a tiny bit taller than Ishtar, but I let the comment wash over me. Nammu was trying to offend me and I didn't intend to give her the satisfaction of reacting to it.

The women swept off to my bedchamber where the chests containing my clothing was stored. Most of them seemed quite merry about the task. I supposed it was an easy job, and perhaps even interesting for them, going through my chests and inspecting my clothing. Over the sound of their chatter and giggles came Nammu's voice, giving strident directions about which items were to be put aside for the sewers and which could be returned to the chests.

"Don't touch that one." Nammu's voice rang out and the chatter stopped. "That is one of my lady's favourites. I will handle that one myself."

Ettu and I looked at each other.

"Which does she think is my favourite?" I whispered to her.

"I'm guessing it's the golden tunic," she whispered back.

We both looked down to her clenched fist concealing the finger ring.

"You don't think…" My words died as Nammu's voice was raised again.

"Who already took this tunic out?" she demanded. "Look at the creases in it."

Murmurs of denial came from the women.

"Someone took it out." Her voice was shrill now. "Who was it?"

Ettu leaned over to whisper in my ear.

"I think we know who planted that finger ring," she said.

CHAPTER 36

The women seemed to take an excessively long time to go through my clothing. When they finally came trooping out, their arms filled with gowns, Nammu's face was sullen.

"I suppose I could try on a couple of items if you need me to," I said.

Perhaps if I could encourage her to linger, she might say something that revealed her guilt.

"Not right now," she said rather shortly. "The sewers will need to see you in them before they begin work. I will arrange a time with Ettu for that."

She said nothing else as she hurried out the door, trailed by the rest of the women.

Ettu, Merytre, Ahmose and I looked at each other.

"Well," I said, then found I didn't know what else to say.

"What are we going to do with this?" Ettu opened her hand to reveal the finger ring.

"I suppose I should take it to Tiye and explain where it was found," I said.

"Not a good idea," she said. "Can you imagine? Hello Tiye, I found your favourite finger ring in my chambers, but I have no idea how it got there."

"I have a pretty good idea," I said.

"And Nammu will deny it," she said.

"No," Merytre said. "She will say you told her to take it."

I started to realise just how much trouble I could be in.

"What if Tiye is behind this?" I asked. "Is it possible she and Nammu have made some kind of alliance and Nammu planted the finger ring for her?"

"I suppose we should assume Lady Tiye is involved," Ettu said. "I have heard rumours about how she came to be Top Ornament."

"They aren't rumours," Merytre said. "I was here when it happened. What she did was… awful."

"I thought Tiye and I had made peace," I said. "But maybe she still feels threatened by me."

"We need to find a way to return it," Ettu said. "Perhaps I could pretend to find it in a public place, like a hallway, or nestled in the grass."

"And if someone sees you?" Ahmose asked. "If they realise you had it all along?"

"You pretend to have found it in a hallway and one of the servants says they swept that hall only moments earlier and it wasn't there," I said. "You could implicate yourself and be accused of the theft."

"We have to get it back to Lady Tiye somehow, " Ettu said. "And I can't think of anything else. Either you give it to her, which we have already agreed is not a good idea, or someone pretends to find it."

"Maybe I could find it," I said. "Surely nobody would accuse me of theft if I suddenly pluck her finger ring out of the grass?"

"Doesn't that still leave us with the same problem?" Merytre asked.

"Yes," Ahmose said. "You say you found it, but a gardener was weeding that exact spot only a few moments earlier."

I twisted around so I could put my feet up on the couch and lie with my head on a cushion. I wanted nothing more than to close my eyes and go to sleep. Forget about all this intrigue for a few hours. But someone needed to make a decision.

"Then I need to tell Tiye the truth," I said. "There doesn't seem to be any other option."

"Let's think about it for a couple of days," Ettu said. "As long as I keep it on me, nobody will find it. If Nammu accuses you and they come to search your chests, it won't be there."

"What if they find something else, though?" Merytre asked. "If Nammu has planted one stolen item, could there be more?"

"We will go through all the clothing chests this afternoon," Ettu said. "You can help me, Merytre. We will make sure there is nothing else hidden away."

"I suppose you should check the jewellery chests too," I said. "I don't know what is in them, so I wouldn't notice if something shouldn't be there."

"We will do that too," she said. "Come, Merytre. We should get started before Nammu has time to make any more trouble."

"I can help," Ahmose said, getting to her feet.

"No," I said. "You have a big night ahead of you. Stay and rest while you can."

Ahmose only shrugged and sat back down. She seemed to doze, despite my pacing of the chamber. My mind whirled with the need for a solution. I went a couple of times to see how Ettu and Merytre were progressing, but they seemed immersed in their task and I didn't want to disturb them. It took them most of the afternoon to check through all the chests, but at last they came to report there was nothing else that shouldn't be there.

"Where is Tiye's finger ring?" I asked.

"I have it here." Ettu showed me a small pouch at her waist. I had noticed most of the women here wore one, although I hadn't stopped to wonder what it was for. "Merytre gave me her spare pouch. The women keep anything that is precious to them in here. Small things mostly, like a lock of hair from a dead child, or a trinket from a beloved friend. Most people don't have much of value, but I suppose they would keep it in their pouch if they did."

"And nobody will have reason to search it?" I asked.

We all looked at Merytre, but she shook her head.

"I can't imagine anyone would do such a thing," she said. "Especially since any accusation would be made against you, my lady, not one of us."

"We have to think of a better place for it soon," I said. "It is too dangerous for you to carry it around."

As the sun set, Ettu lit the lamps and Ahmose made her final preparations.

"If I can get to them, do you have a message for Tall and Half?" she asked me.

She waited, bottle in her hand, ready to drink her potion. A sack containing the ingredients she would need to make two more doses waited beside the door.

"Tell them I will demand they be returned to me as soon as I meet with Pharaoh," I said. "Find out if they are well and make sure they know not to risk trying to send a message except through you."

"Anything else?" she asked.

They had probably already guessed I was confined to the Palace of the Ornaments. The news that I wasn't to be queen after all would probably come as no surprise, to Tall at least, and perhaps by now he had managed to convey that information to Half. They wouldn't care about the matter of Tiye's ring, although Nammu's treachery might interest them, and they didn't know Nebtu so her disappearance wouldn't be important to them.

"Just ask what news they have for me," I said.

Ahmose touched her fingers to her lips, then drank her potion. I studied her carefully, hoping to see some sign of its effects. A shimmer perhaps, or an unevenness around her edges.

But once again, I saw nothing. She had said she would only be invisible to the ones the potion was directed at, but it still disappointed me to see no evidence of it.

Ahmose took her sack and left. I sat on a couch and tried not to fidget. All I could do now was pray to Marduk for her safe return.

CHAPTER 37

A knock came at the door, loud and officious. I froze. Ettu's fingers strayed to her pouch, as if to reassure herself the finger ring was still there, before she answered the door.

"I need to speak to the Lady Kassaya," came a male voice.

From my perch on the couch, I couldn't see who it was until Ettu opened the door wider.

"My lady."

Panouk bowed deeply, giving me a good view of his bald scalp. It shone in the lamp light and I wondered whether he had oiled it or if his head was sweating. I restrained a giggle. The chief administrator didn't look like the type of man who would have a sense of humour, particularly when it came to matters about his own appearance.

"Administrator," I said. "Can I help you with something?"

"I am afraid I need to search your chambers," he said.

My heart sank and I prayed he hadn't noticed any change in my expression.

"Is this a joke?" I asked.

"Unfortunately not. Lady Tiye has reported the theft of two items from her chambers."

"Two?"

"You are aware of the matter?" His eyes narrowed, as if I was suddenly of even greater suspicion than before.

"I heard she claimed a finger ring was missing. I wasn't aware of a second item."

"Subsequent to the disappearance of the finger ring, she has now discovered another jewel has been stolen."

"And is it usual practice to search the chambers of other Ornaments when one claims to have lost something?" My tone was frosty. Indignance seemed as good a defence as anything else.

"Only when a witness comes forward to say they have found stolen property in those chambers."

"What?" I gaped at him, too surprised to conceal my reaction.

"I am afraid one of your lady's maids has turned over an item she found hidden in your clothing chests this afternoon. That gives me cause to search your chambers for the other missing jewel."

"Who is this maid and what is it she claims to have found?"

I studiously avoided looking at Ettu, not wanting to give Panouk any reason to be suspicious of her.

"Nammu," he said. "And this is what she found."

He showed me a pendant of lapis lazuli. It was cut in the shape of a tear drop and polished to a high sheen.

"It is a very fine piece," I said. "But I have never seen it before. She certainly didn't get it from my chambers."

"Unfortunately she claims she did. I am sure you can see my predicament."

"I'm not sure what predicament would cause you to take the word of a servant over that of an Ornament."

"When the servant can produce evidence of her claim, which in this case, she has, the situation requires investigation. And it is well known that you and Lady Tiye have had a... confrontation."

"She locked me in and refused to let me out until I cleaned her piss-soaked bathing chamber." I immediately regretted my outburst. We had made a treaty, after all, and sounding aggrieved at Tiye wouldn't help my case.

"What occurs between Ornaments is nothing to do with me, except where matters progress to a more serious level, such as theft. And I'm sure you are aware the Lady Tiye is Pharaoh's Favourite. It behoves me to treat her in the manner she expects, and she has specifically requested your chambers be searched."

"Nammu is lying about having found it in my chambers. She stole it herself, or got it from whoever stole it."

Panouk shrugged.

"We can stand here and argue about it all night, my lady, or I can get on with searching your chambers," he said. "Please stand aside and allow me to do my job. I would not like to have to restrain you for your own safety."

"Restrain me?" My voice was high now. "Are you threatening me, Administrator?"

"I am afraid that if you were to become hysterical, as does happen with some of the more overwrought Ornaments, I would have to ensure you don't injure yourself before you calm down. I am sure you want to avoid that as much as I do."

"So if I don't allow you to search my chambers, you will claim I was hysterical and lock me away so you can do what you want?" I asked.

He only looked at me and made no reply. I sighed.

"Fine. Search my chambers. You will find nothing, because I have stolen nothing. And when you are finished, you can tell Nammu she is dismissed immediately from my employment. I expect her to be turned out of the Palace."

"I believe she has already accepted employment with the Lady Tiye," Panouk said. "A reward for her honesty in returning the stolen gem."

I swallowed the angry words that wanted to come out of my

mouth and went to stand at the window. I stared out at the dark landscape and tried to compose myself. My hands were shaking and my heart raced. This was clearly Nammu's revenge for not being offered her own bedchamber, but Tiye must also be involved. How else would Nammu have procured a second jewel so quickly?

Panouk brought in several servants. I hadn't realised they were waiting outside in the hallway. How much had they overheard? What gossip would be spread about me now?

It took them a couple of hours to search my chambers thoroughly. Servants brought our evening meal as usual, but the savoury aromas turned my stomach. Neither Ettu nor Merytre ate, although I told them they should if they were hungry. Just because Panouk was rifling through my things didn't mean they should go without food.

Eventually the servants filed out and Panouk returned to the sitting chamber.

"Find anything?" I asked snidely.

"No, my lady, I am pleased to say we didn't," he said. "I now need to search your person, and also your lady's maids."

I couldn't let him near Ettu.

"Absolutely not," I said. "I have tolerated this nonsense for long enough. You have already pawed through everything in my chambers. I refuse to let you put your hands on me as well, or my lady's maids."

"I am afraid I must insist," he said.

"No."

I glared at him. Surely as an Ornament, I must have some kind of power here.

"If you refuse, I will have you removed to a holding cell and confined there while we summon the police chief. I would much prefer the situation didn't need to be escalated in such a way, but you leave me with no other option."

"This is absurd. I have done nothing and you have no

evidence of any wrongdoing, other than the word of a vindictive servant."

"Lady Tiye has requested a thorough investigation into the matter of her stolen jewels and I do not intend to have her report to Pharaoh that I failed to do my duty. I am sure you can appreciate that."

"I appreciate nothing of your presence here today. Kindly remove yourself from my chambers at once."

But if I had thought bluffing would unnerve him, I was wrong. He only went to the doorway and gestured outside. In came three men who hadn't entered earlier with the servants. He must have left them waiting out there in case he needed them. One was Amankhau, but I didn't know the other two.

"Restrain her please," Panouk said. "I am afraid she has become hysterical and is talking nonsense. We cannot search her while she is in such a state. She will need to be moved to a holding cell until the police chief can get here."

"Do not put your hands on me," I warned them, but Amankhau and another man took hold of my arms.

"It would be better for you if you walk, my lady," Amankhau said. "Although we will carry you if we must."

"I will lodge a complaint against all four of you," I said. "I will make my complaint directly to Pharaoh."

"Very good," Panouk said. "Take her away so we can conclude this nasty business. Once she is confined safely, send for the police chief. She is not to be searched until he arrives. I want no suggestion that we have acted inappropriately."

As they led me through the door and out into the hallway, I heard Panouk speak to Ettu and Merytre.

"Now then," he said. "Are you going to be more sensible than your mistress?"

CHAPTER 38

They locked me in a chamber which was surely too small to have ever been anyone's bedchamber. I guessed it might once have been used for storage, although it held nothing now other than a low stool, a lamp, and a rug. There wasn't even a window.

"I will have refreshments brought for you." Amankhau's tone was conversational, as if it was perfectly normal for him to lock an Ornament in a storage chamber and send her melon juice and bread.

"I will see to it that you lose your position for this," I said. "I will submit a complaint directly to Pharaoh."

"Yes, yes. You will do as you must. But for now, I'm afraid we need to keep you here for your safety."

He lit the lamp and closed the door behind him. I tried the doorknob, but it was locked. I waited a few moments to give him time to leave, then pounded on the door in case someone passing might let me out. But if anyone heard, they didn't respond.

Not knowing what else to do, I sat on the stool. It was a plain wooden thing with three legs, sturdy but hardly comfortable. The air in the chamber was already stuffy and sweat trickled down the back of my neck. My hands shook and I took a few deep breaths to calm myself. Panouk had surely already searched both Ettu and Merytre. Had he discovered the jewel hidden in Ettu's pouch? Had she, too, been locked up or, worse, expelled from the Palace? Surely they wouldn't physically harm her.

If she was accused of theft, would she be entitled to a trial? I suddenly realised I knew nothing of the laws here. Our lessons with Ahmose had covered little more than that whatever Pharaoh said was law, and the Palace seemed to operate to its own rules. Even if there was a trial and I was permitted to speak as a witness, I didn't actually *see* Nammu do anything, so my word might be of little benefit to Ettu.

Perhaps Ahmose's knowledge of secret things included a potion to make someone tell the truth. We could make Nammu drink it and she would confess to having stolen both jewels in an attempt to get revenge on me. As soon as they released me and Ahmose returned, we would find a way to force Nammu to tell the truth.

I felt a little better now I had a plan. Even if Ahmose didn't have a truth spell, there would be something else she could do. Maybe she could sneak Ettu an invisibility potion and smuggle her out of the Palace. Or I could drink the potion myself and go to Pharaoh. I could tell him about the injustices being carried out here and he would surely want an accounting from Panouk and Amankhau for their actions.

So there were several ways I might help Ettu. But right now, the only thing I could do was wait. The lamp burned low and my bladder became increasingly uncomfortable. My stomach growled and there was no sign of the promised refreshments. Perhaps Amankhau had heard me pounding on the door and feared I would try to escape if he sent food to me.

Eventually I heard footsteps in the hallway and the door rattled as it was unlocked.

"I do apologise for such a long wait." Amankhau's tone was

insincere, even if his words were correct. "You are free to return to your chambers."

"I assume you found nothing," I said, praying to Marduk I was right.

"Quite the contrary," he said. "It seems Nammu was mistaken about who took the jewel."

My heart rose. Ettu was safe.

"We found it on your lady's maid and she has already given a full confession. She admitted you had no knowledge of her theft."

"What nonsense. None of my maids would do such a thing."

Careful. Don't mention Ettu's name or he will know you already knew.

"I'm afraid that is the case. Ettu says she stole the jewel to get revenge on Lady Tiye for perceived slights against you."

"That is false. I want to speak with Ettu immediately."

"Unfortunately that will not be possible. She has already been removed from the Palace and will be imprisoned. A trial hardly seems necessary, given she has confessed and the jewel was found in her possession, but she will face a magistrate as is her right."

"There must be a mistake," I said. "I told you Nammu took the jewel herself."

"And yet it was found on the person of one of your lady's maids. One who, I hear, you are particularly close to."

"What is that supposed to mean?" I didn't like the sly turn in his voice.

Amankhau shrugged, seemingly trying to give the impression it was no more than a casual thought. He gestured for me to exit the chamber.

"A devoted lady's maid would, I expect, do anything her mistress asked of her," he said when I didn't move.

"Are you implying I asked Ettu to steal the jewel for me?" I gave him a hard look. "That would be a dangerous thing for you to suggest, since it directly accuses me."

"Perhaps you stole it yourself and told her to hide it for you."

I glared at him, using the moment to compose myself. Was this Amankhau's revenge because I complained to Panouk about Tall and Half never reaching the stables? I needed to tread very carefully.

"I did no such thing and I find your suggestion offensive to the extreme," I said. "My father will hear of this and so will Pharaoh."

"You should be careful." Amankhau's tone turned nasty. "You have already made a name for yourself as a trouble maker. Asking too many questions. Poking around in things that are none of your business. Women like you tend to get themselves into trouble."

I could only gape at him. What in Marduk's name was he talking about? Was this because I had been asking about Nebtu? Was it intended as a warning that I should keep my questions to myself?

"Do you intend to stand here all night?" he asked. "I have other things to do, but if you will follow me, I will escort you back to your chambers."

"I demand to speak with Ettu."

"As I said, that is not possible."

"Then make it possible."

We glared at each other. I was acutely aware that if I backed down now, it would signal I could be intimidated. I couldn't let that happen. Whether this was intended as payback for complaining about him or as a warning to stop asking questions, I needed to get the upper hand.

"I'm beginning to suspect you orchestrated this whole plot yourself," I said. "You stole the jewels, perhaps thinking they wouldn't be missed. After all, Pharaoh's Favourite surely has so many jewels, she would hardly notice if one or two disappeared. But she did notice and you panicked. What did you promise Nammu in exchange for her claiming to have found one of the missing jewels in my chambers? Gems to keep for herself? An introduction to Pharaoh?"

He spluttered, seemingly unable to string any coherent words together. He hadn't expected such an accusation.

"If you don't release Ettu immediately, I will tell every Ornament in this place what you did. After all, if you are successful in targeting one of us, you'll do it again. Maybe you've even done it before. I will ask around about what has happened when things have gone missing previously. When the entire Palace rises up against you, you will lose your position and I will personally make sure your chambers are thoroughly searched before you can secret away anything else you have stolen."

"Preposterous," he finally managed.

"You have until I get through that doorway to make your decision."

I pushed past him. Just as my sandal touched the floor outside, he spoke.

"I will have your lady's maid released," he said. "But you will have to explain to Lady Tiye yourself. Panouk has already told her an arrest has been made and I doubt she will be pleased to learn the thief has been released without charge."

"I will speak with Tiye, but I want Ettu returned to my chambers first. You have one hour to facilitate her return. If I don't see her by then, I'll be talking to every Ornament I can find and asking them to spread the word of your thefts."

I swept away down the hallway. My hands shook, my knees trembled, and I couldn't catch my breath. But I had done it. I had secured Ettu's release. Amankhau would make me pay for it, though. If he wasn't my enemy before, he certainly was now.

CHAPTER 39

Merytre was in the sitting chamber when I arrived. She jumped up from the couch and rushed to greet me.

"Oh, my lady," she breathed. "You won't believe what happened."

"I heard Amankhau's version," I said. "But tell me what you saw. I am not convinced he was entirely truthful with me."

"They made an awful mess when they searched your chambers. Left your clothes strewn everywhere. I'm sorry, I just realised should have been cleaning it all up while I waited for you, but I was too worried to think of it."

Her mouth wobbled and she looked like she was about to burst into tears.

"It's all right," I said. "I can help you clean it up later. Tell me the rest."

"Panouk was much nastier after you left. He was very mad they didn't find the missing finger ring and he was sure it was somewhere in your chambers. He searched me first. I didn't argue since I had nothing to hide, but maybe I should have. Maybe if I had argued, he wouldn't have searched Ettu as well."

"He would have done it anyway. He was determined to find some sort of evidence and he didn't intend leaving without it."

"I think he was rather disappointed he didn't find anything on me. Then he went to Ettu. She tried to argue with him, to tell him he had no legal right to put his hands on her body. He just laughed and said since she wasn't an Ornament, there were no restrictions about who touched her, and Pharaoh left it up to him to manage the Palace however he saw fit."

"And he found the finger ring in her pouch?"

Merytre put her hand over her mouth and nodded. I waited while she composed herself.

"He was almost gleeful when he found it. He cried out, aha, I knew it was here, and he held it up so we could all see it."

"What did Ettu do?"

"Oh, she was amazing. She merely held her head high and told him she had never seen it before. She accused Panouk of having it in his hand when he searched her pouch."

"Clever girl," I said.

I wasn't sure I would have had the presence of mind to say such a thing if I was in Ettu's position. But her words would work well with the defence I had already established for her. I could say the administrators were working together to steal from the Ornaments.

"Amankhau had come back by then and Panouk told him to take Ettu away. Amankhau grabbed her arm and dragged her from the chamber. I've heard nothing since then. I don't even know where he took her."

"She was imprisoned," I said. "Amankhau said she confessed to having stolen the finger ring."

Merytre looked surprised.

"If she did, it wasn't while she was here," she said. "They must have wrung it out of her after they took her away."

"Whether it's true she confessed or not, she should be returned to us shortly," I said, and told her how I had secured

Ettu's release. "And if she isn't, you and I will go tell everyone the administrators are stealing from the Ornaments and framing other women for the thefts."

"That is a very clever plan," she said. "But…"

Her voice trailed away. I waited for her to continue, but she only pursed her lips.

"But what?" I asked.

"Are you sure you want to go to so much effort for a servant? She can be easily replaced, and you have caused a lot of trouble for yourself. Panouk and Amankhau are powerful men."

"I don't care about any of that. I only care about getting Ettu released. We all know how that jewel really came to be in my chambers and I won't allow one of my lady's maids to be imprisoned for something she didn't do."

"I don't think there is a single other Ornament who would do what you have for a servant." Merytre blinked rapidly, as if fighting back tears.

It was only when she said that, I realised I had been thinking of Ettu as a friend, not my servant. I must never forget her loyalty to me was because of the agreement we had made, not because she was my friend.

"Well, that's a shame," I said. "Perhaps if folk were a little kinder to each other, there wouldn't be so many unhappy women here."

"What makes you think anyone is unhappy?" Merytre asked. "We live in a fine palace and have plenty of food. We get to wear the clothes our mistresses no longer want, and we aren't required to do physical labour, like planting or harvesting. This is a safe place, for most of us."

Her voice trailed away and I guessed that she, like me, was thinking about Nebtu.

"But nobody seems happy," I said. "There is a lot to be said for having food and shelter, but what about joy? Peace?"

"I suppose the Ornaments are not here for joy or peace, and

neither are the servants. The likes of you are here to entertain Pharaoh and produce sons for him. The likes of me are here to make your life comfortable while you do so. Nobody expects to be happy as well."

"Why shouldn't we expect happiness? Or contentment at least?"

"I think most of the Ornaments *are* content, my lady."

Was it only me who felt stifled by not being allowed to leave the grounds or even to be alone? Before I could ponder this further, the door opened and Ettu was there.

"Ettu!" I said. "Thank Marduk."

I had expected she would be pale and teary after her ordeal, but she looked more tired than anything else.

"My lady, I believe I have you to thank for my release," she said. "I must warn you, though, Amankhau is most displeased about it."

"Amankhau is a bully," I said. "And I don't care in the slightest if he is unhappy with me. I am just thankful you have been released."

"Panouk still has the finger ring," she said. "I think he intends to return it to Lady Tiye himself."

"I will speak with her," I said. "This nonsense has gone too far."

"I think you underestimate the level of competition amongst the Ornaments," Ettu said. "Merytre would know more about it than I do, but from what I have heard, it wouldn't be the first time an Ornament has pretended something was stolen from her."

"It happens from time to time," Merytre said. "Usually for attention, I think. But in this case, it could be Lady Tiye's way of seeking revenge. I doubt she has forgiven you for refusing to clean her bathing chamber."

I would confront Tiye, although the most likely outcome

would probably be that she claimed ignorance of Nammu's plot. Tiye could be either a powerful enemy or a powerful friend. I would give her the chance to decide which she would be.

CHAPTER 40

*O*nce again I spent the night in the sitting chamber, waiting for Ahmose to return. Ettu said she would wait with me, but I insisted she go to bed. She'd had a traumatic day, what with being arrested and threatened with Marduk-only-knew-what. Merytre stayed with me for a while, but when I caught her trying to stifle a yawn for the third time, I sent her to her bed as well.

The lamp cast a warm glow over the sitting room and I tucked my feet beneath me on the couch. My eyes were heavy and I kept waking with a start when my head dropped. I wished I could speak with Tiye and resolve the nonsense about her stolen jewels, but it was far too late to go visiting. At length, I could stay awake no longer and lay down, a cushion beneath my head. I woke when the door opened.

Ahmose's face was lined with weariness and her shoulders slumped as if she could barely hold herself up.

"Sit," I said, getting up to help her to a chair.

She eased herself into it, knees cracking as she did. I brought her a mug of beer and she touched her fingers to her lips in gratitude. I held my tongue as she drank, although I was bursting to know what news she brought.

"I found them," she said when she had finally drained the mug. "They are safe enough."

"Thank you, Marduk," I whispered. "Are they in Pharaoh's palace? Did you have any trouble with the guards? Tell me everything."

Ettu and Merytre appeared in the doorway in their night-clothes. I was pleased to see Ettu already looked less pale. They both came to sit down and I poured Ahmose another mug of beer.

"I had to wait quite a while before the guards here opened the gates," she said. "I was starting to wonder how else I might get out if they didn't have reason to open them before morning, but finally a messenger came."

"They let in a man?" I asked sharply. "I thought that wasn't permitted."

"He had a message for Amankhau, from what I heard," Ahmose said. "I suppose the rules might be different for the likes of him. Anyway, they finally opened the gates and I was able to slip through before they closed them again. I walked to Pharaoh's palace and hid behind some bushes until I got a good look at the guards. Then I mixed up a new potion and drank it. There were lots of folk going in and out, and the guards had left the door ajar so they didn't have to keep opening them."

"That doesn't sound very secure," Ettu said.

"It was fortunate for me, though," Ahmose said. "Once I was inside, nobody challenged me. I heard music and carousing, and I followed the sound until I reached a banquet hall. It was some sort of celebration, with hundreds of people eating and drinking. There were dancers, acrobats, and musicians, and nobody took any notice of an old woman who wandered in and found a spot to sit. I helped myself to some food and watched for Tall and Half."

"What did you eat?" Merytre asked.

"Nothing particularly fancy, given it seemed to be a banquet. I suppose Pharaoh and the like ate richer foods, but where I sat, it was roasted pig, bread, and beer. I saw servants with bottles of wine, but they never brought them down as far as I was."

"Did you see Pharaoh?" I asked.

"I heard he was there, right down the other end, but there were too many folk for me to catch even a glimpse of him."

I hadn't seen him yet either and he was supposed to be my husband. I had an image in my mind of what I expected him to look like, based on the men I saw around me. Tall and broad shouldered, shaved bald, and with firm muscles. But still, I would like to see him for myself.

"I heard someone talking about a halfwit who was to tell jokes for Pharaoh," Ahmose continued.

"Half," I breathed.

"Yes," she said. "I thought it too much of a coincidence to be anything else. So I started making my way around the edges of the banquet hall. I figured if Half was there somewhere, Tall might also be nearby."

"And you found them?" I asked, unable to wait any longer. Her tale was taking too long.

"I did indeed," she said. "Or rather, Tall found me. I heard him call out Teacher and when I turned, there he was."

"Did he look well?" I asked.

"Perfectly fine. He has put on a little weight. They must be eating well. He took me to the chamber he and Half share, and we waited there until Half finished his performance for Pharaoh."

She stopped to take a deep drink and when she set the mug down again, Ettu got up to refill it this time.

"Thank you," Ahmose said to her. "I have walked a very long way tonight and find myself still thirsty."

A demand for her to hurry up wanted to burst out of my

mouth. I distracted myself by clenching my fists until my nails dug into my palms.

"I told Tall you sent me and he said careful," she said. "I think it was intended as a message for you, my lady."

"Was that all he said?" I asked.

"No, there were two other words. Pharaoh and danger."

I could hear Tall's voice saying those words. Careful! Pharaoh! Danger! It would have been in Babylonian, of course, since he was unable to make himself speak in Egyptian. Clearly he wanted to warn me of some danger, but did he mean the danger was from Pharaoh, or that Pharaoh was involved in some other way?

"Were his words in that exact order?" I asked. "Careful, Pharaoh, danger."

"Yes," Ahmose said. "He repeated them twice more in the same order."

"I wonder if the order is significant," Ettu said.

"I don't understand," Merytre said. "If he has a message for you, why didn't he send the whole thing? Does he not know he can trust Ahmose?"

"That is how he speaks," I told her. "Usually I can understand him, but I'm not sure what he means this time."

"It is obviously a warning," Ettu said.

"Yes, but of what?" I asked. "Ahmose, what else did you learn?"

"When Half returned, he told me that the night we arrived here, they were escorted straight to the front gates and turned out."

"Liars," I muttered. Both Panouk and Amankhau had insisted the two men spent the night in the stables. What else did they lie about to the residents here?

"Half said they heard the man who was sent with them tell the guards the administrator wanted to know why they were let in. The guards said Tall and Half obviously weren't proper men, so they didn't think the prohibition against men entering the grounds applied to them."

Anger welled within me, but I didn't let myself say anything, not wanting to interrupt Ahmose's story. Ettu had no such compunction, muttering a stream of angry words to herself. Merytre only looked confused, but of course, she hadn't met Tall and Half. She wouldn't realise this was how most folk treated them.

"They didn't know what else to do, so they walked back to the Palace," Ahmose said. "The guards recognised them and one asked if their lady had sent them as gifts for Pharaoh. Half knew it was a joke, but he said that yes, they were gifts and their lady hoped Pharaoh would find them amusing. The guards allowed them into the palace."

"That was very quick thinking," I said.

"He is a clever man," Ettu said.

"Nobody else took any notice of them, so they simply found a bedchamber that didn't seem to be in use and went to sleep," Ahmose said. "The next morning, they learned where the servants ate and began to integrate themselves."

"And nobody stopped them?" I asked.

"Half said folk tend to either not see him or to laugh at him, and this was no different," Ahmose said. "I suppose it was the same for Tall."

Ettu shook her head a little, but she kept whatever she thought of this to herself.

"Half heard that Pharaoh was holding a banquet, so he went along and introduced himself to one of the administrators. The man presented him to Pharaoh and Half told a few jokes. Apparently Pharaoh found him very amusing and said he could stay for as long as he was funny."

A weight slid off my shoulders. They were safe, for now at least. I couldn't bear not knowing whether they had somewhere to sleep. But they had a bedchamber and food and a job of sorts.

"He had other news too," Ahmose said. "The administrator he

spoke to said Pharaoh was planning to visit the Palace of the Ornaments in five days. That was three days ago."

"So he will be here tomorrow?" I asked.

She nodded. "Assuming Half's information is correct."

"Does he know why Pharaoh is coming?"

Did I dare hope he came to meet me at last?

"He visits regularly," she said. "Usually at least once a week, although apparently it has been a couple of weeks since his last visit as he went to a town called Dendera for some religious festival."

"Oh, my lady," Ettu breathed. "We must figure out what you will wear."

"Will I be given any official notice, I wonder?" I mused. "Or does he just show up?"

"I assume the administrators would be advised of an impending visit," Ahmose said. "They would need to make arrangements. Food, security."

"Merytre, do you know anything else?" I asked.

"Sometimes I have heard ahead of time that Pharaoh is to visit," she said. "But usually not. I suspect certain Ornaments might get told, though. Lady Tiye, in particular, always seems especially well presented when Pharaoh visits, even when nobody else knows he is coming."

"What about Tall's message?" Ettu asked. "Did Half know anything more about that?"

"I didn't get to ask him," Ahmose said. "It was late by the time he returned to their bedchamber and we only had time to talk briefly. But there was one other thing he said."

She hesitated.

"Go on," I said.

"Half thinks Nammu knew when we left Babylon that you wouldn't be queen."

"I guessed as much," I said.

Tall had tried to tell me, but in hindsight it was obvious. The snide comments, the sniggers. The way neither Nammu nor Belet-ili seemed particularly concerned with being in my good favour as we travelled. It all made sense.

"Marduk," Ettu said. "Ishtar must have told her. I swear, my lady, I knew nothing about it."

I waved away her protest and nodded for Ahmose to continue.

"Half overheard Nammu and Belet-ili talking while we sailed on the Great River," Ahmose said. "They didn't explicitly say it, but there were enough hints for him to piece it together. He was trying to tell you when we arrived in Thebes, but there was no chance to speak with you privately, and he didn't want to say it in front of everyone in case he was wrong and embarrassed you."

"Did you learn anything else?" I asked.

"That was all we had time for," Ahmose said. "I had to leave or risk the potion wearing off before I could get back. I didn't want to take the last dose unless I absolutely had to."

Her gamble had bought us valuable information. I wondered how long we should wait before she went again.

rose early the next morning, but Ettu and Merytre were already up and planning what I would wear for Pharaoh's visit. They had laid out the golden tunic and had selected a wig and various items of jewellery.

"You don't think I should dress like the other Ornaments do?" I asked.

There were women of many nationalities living in the Palace and I didn't stick out any more than anyone else when I wore the same clothes as they did. But this gown made me look distinctly foreign.

"You are a Princess of Babylon," Ettu said fiercely. "And I think you should look like one when you first meet Pharaoh."

Merytre nodded and I decided not to argue. She had lived in the Palace for years and had served a number of Ornaments. If she thought Ettu was wrong, she wouldn't be nodding.

"I should try to speak with Tiye first," I said. "We need to sort out this business with her stolen jewels."

"She will be busy preparing for Pharaoh's visit," Merytre said. "I doubt she will make time to see you today."

"Tomorrow," Ettu said. "Give her a day to calm down."

It seemed more prudent to deal with the situation immediately, but I let them persuade me. By the time the rest of my lady's maids arrived — without Nammu — Ettu and Merytre had already bathed me and shaved me all over yet again. I wore the golden tunic and a wig with tight curls all over the front half of my head and braids at the back that hung to my shoulders. I sat on a stool as Merytre made up my face with thick lines of kohl that extended well past my eyes and far too much colour on my cheeks and lips.

"Have you heard?" one of the women said to Merytre. "Pharaoh is to visit today."

I hadn't bothered to get to know their names, these indistinguishable women who appeared only to bathe and dress me, then disappeared again until the next morning. It hadn't occurred to me until now to wonder whether I was supposed to be occupying them with other tasks during the day. Were all my lady's maids supposed to attend to me all day, like Ettu and Merytre did? After all, I wasn't supposed to be left alone. But I didn't ask, not wanting to endure being surrounded by a gaggle of women all day. I would go out of my mind if I had to listen to their chatter for any longer than I already did.

The women argued over whether my outfit was the best choice for Pharaoh's visit and criticised Merytre's hand in applying my kohl.

"Where is Nammu?" someone asked and was quickly shushed.

So word had gotten out that something had happened with Nammu, but did they know the details? How much of what they had heard was truth and how much was more of Nammu's lies? It was only then I noticed Belet-ili towards the back of the group. I hadn't heard her voice once today, but I didn't doubt she was busy listening to everything that was said so she could report it all back to Nammu.

I debated whether to speak to her. I could be stern and ask whether she had been involved in Nammu's plot and demand she tell me what else she knew. But I likely wouldn't get anything useful out of her and she would tell Nammu I knew the truth about her deception. It might be more useful to let her think I didn't know, or that I didn't think she was involved. I might perhaps be able to feed some misinformation back to Nammu before Belet-ili realised. I waited until the other women were leaving, before I called her to me.

"Belet-ili," I said. "Come talk with me."

She seemed to startle, as if she had thought I didn't know she was there. I saw the way she hunched her shoulders as she pushed through the chattering women. Gone was the confident swagger she usually had in Nammu's presence. Alone, she was insecure. As she reached me, I gave her my best attempt at a friendly smile.

"I have hardly seen you since we arrived," I said. "Are your accommodations suitable?"

"Oh, yes, my lady," she stammered, seemingly disconcerted. "I am sharing a chamber with three other lady's maids. We each have a bed and a chest for our clothes. And there is a bathing chamber just down the hallway."

"Where do you eat your meals?"

"In the servants' dining hall, my lady. There is always food there, since we all keep different hours depending on when our mistress needs us. The food is basic but plentiful."

"That's good to hear."

I was momentarily lost for words. What else should I ask? I wanted to give the appearance of being genuinely concerned for her welfare and comfort.

"Have you made any friends here?" I asked.

She hesitated and seemed to choose her words carefully.

"There hasn't really been time for such things," she said.

"When we are not needed by our mistress, we are required to work at other tasks. Weaving or sewing, depending on our abilities. Those women who can't do either help in the kitchens or with cleaning. A lot of work goes into making the Palace run efficiently. I am adequate enough at weaving, but I am better at sewing and that's where I have been assigned."

"What kind of things do you sew?"

"At the moment, I am stitching hems. Tapestries, curtains, bed sheets. Whatever needs to be hemmed. I have been promised more interesting work in a few weeks once I have proved myself with basic sewing."

"That sounds very good for you," I said.

At least she was being kept busy, although it was a pity it was at a task where she was also free to gossip as she worked. Maybe I could get her moved to a different role, perhaps cleaning or cooking. One where she would have to work harder with less time for gossip.

"My lady." She hesitated, as if unsure whether to continue. "Have I done something to displease you?"

"Why do you ask?"

"I notice you still have a spare chamber. Both Ettu and Ahmose have been given accommodation within your suite, but not me."

Did she know Nammu had already asked? Surely they would have discussed it. I chose my words carefully.

"Ettu and Ahmose have both proved their worth to me," I said. "What have you done that would make me inclined to reward you with your own bedchamber?"

She flushed and stammered. I guessed she had expected me to make excuses, rather than ask her to account for her own actions. Maybe she really didn't know Nammu had already asked the same thing.

"Go now," I said, before she managed to say anything coherent. "If you prove your worth to me, I will consider giving you the spare chamber. But until then, you are no more to me than the other lady's maids who attend me in the mornings."

Her cheeks went an even darker red and she fled without another word. Had I convinced her to do something to show she was loyal to me or had I only made another enemy?

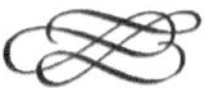

CHAPTER 42

At last, only Ettu, Merytre and Ahmose were left in my chambers. Merytre passed me a hand mirror and I studied how she had elongated my eyes with kohl and somehow made me look more alluring. In fact, I almost looked pretty. Not beautiful like Ishtar, but not quite as plain as usual. It was a foreign kind of beauty, though, with the kohl and the hair that wasn't my own.

A servant woman came to announce Pharaoh's impending visit. All residents were to gather in the main courtyard before the sun reached its peak, she said. Pharaoh would address us all.

"We should go now, my lady," Merytre said. "Everyone will be rushing to get there and secure a good position."

"The sun won't be at its peak for another couple of hours yet."

I was unenthusiastic about the prospect of standing out in the heat for so long.

"If you aren't there early, you won't be close enough to see him," she warned.

I sighed. Surely I would see him afterwards. He would summon his newest "wife" for a private audience so we could finally meet.

"Let's go then," I said.

The hallways were still empty as we made our way to the courtyard.

"Where is everyone?" I asked.

"They are likely still dressing, my lady," Merytre said. "We had advance notice from Ahmose, but most of the women here wouldn't have known until a servant brought the news to them."

Hopefully that meant I would secure a good position in the courtyard.

We soon encountered other Ornaments heading in the same direction.

"Either their lady's maids worked very fast or they too had advance warning," Ettu muttered to me.

I was about to agree with her when I spotted Tiye. She was some distance ahead of us and didn't seem to have noticed me yet.

"No doubt Tiye already knew," I said.

"Will you speak with her today?"

"If I have an opportunity. Otherwise, I will see her tomorrow."

"She probably won't believe you had nothing to do with the theft."

"I'm not yet convinced she had nothing to do with it either."

It was a long walk, and by the time we reached the courtyard dozens of Ornaments already waited there with their servants. I supposed they must be the ones whose chambers were located on this side of the Palace. Henutmire was there and gave me a friendly smile. Gilukhipa frowned and Ineni turned her back when she saw me. So word of my "theft" had obviously gone out and the Ornaments were choosing who to ally themselves with. It was no surprise if they sided with Tiye, of course. They hardly knew me.

The courtyard was a large area paved with mud bricks and circled by tall, stone pillars. A dais at one end bore an enormous golden throne. There was no roof and the sun beat down mercilessly. Merytre led us to a spot close to the dais, where there was a pillar I could lean against and which might provide a little shade as the sun moved.

The courtyard filled with Ornaments dressed in their finest and trailed by their lady's maids. Some seemed to bring all their maids and others only two or three. I saw a number of faces I recognised, women I passed in the hallways each day, but there were many others I didn't. Every nationality I could think of was represented and there were many women whose origins I couldn't place from their appearance. A tall black woman with a haughty face intrigued me and I wondered who she was. A woman who might have been Greek — her glossy black hair was surely her own and not a wig — gave me a tentative smile, then quickly looked away as if she already regretted it.

The sun crawled through the sky, warming the air and the mud brick floor. Heat radiated off the pillar beside me, although I was reluctant to move away from it and perhaps lose the chance of a little shade later. The constant chatter of the women around me frayed my nerves and the overpowering aroma of so many different kinds of oils and perfumes made my head pound and my nose run. After enduring this for an hour, I almost didn't care about waiting to meet Pharaoh. I just wanted to be away from all the noise and the smell and the heat.

"How much longer?" I muttered to Merytre.

She shrugged. "We never know exactly when he will arrive. Sometimes he comes early, as if to catch the Ornaments unawares. Other times he keeps them waiting all day and only arrives at sunset."

"Marduk, I hope he doesn't do that today."

I waved my hand in front of my face, trying to get a little air moving to cool me. Sweat trickled down my neck and dampness spread beneath my armpits. I hoped I would have time to change before meeting Pharaoh. At this rate, I would be a sweaty, disgusting mess by the time he arrived. Not the impression I wanted to make, especially when I was surrounded by so many beautiful and immaculately presented women.

We waited for several hours and my feet were aching before I finally spotted movement. A squad of guards surrounded the dais, spears held upright and daggers poking from their waistbands. So it seemed the rule against weapons inside the palace didn't apply to Pharaoh's own men.

A loud blast of music made me jump. In came two men wielding enormous silver trumpets. They took up positions on each side of the dais and continued the celebratory noise on their instruments. Each blast sent another stabbing pain through my head.

Half a dozen scantily clad women were the next to enter. They positioned themselves in front of the dais, sitting elegantly with their feet tucked beneath them. If they felt the day's heat, they showed no sign of it. I eyed their sheer garments and tried to push down my disgust. Did Pharaoh really think it appropriate to bring such women to the place where his "wives" lived? Was this the kind of man Father had sent me to — one who needed to be surrounded by half-naked women at all times?

At last, the trumpets fell silent and so did the chatter in the courtyard. This, it seemed, was an indication of Pharaoh's imminent arrival. More guards filed in, or maybe they were soldiers. I couldn't tell the difference, if indeed there was any. Twenty men, then behind them came another man. Towering above the heads of the soldiers I could make out a tall, white crown. This was him. He was coming. I was finally about to see my husband for the first time.

The man who followed the guards could most generously be described as portly. His enormous belly sagged over the belt of his *shendyt* and his arms were flabby. He was shirtless, as most of the men here were, with his chest covered only by an oversized lapis lazuli collar. I was close enough to see his puffy face and how his jowls wobbled when he walked. He had a strange prancing gait that seemed at odds with his solemn face.

My heart sank. Surely this couldn't be him? But he made his way onto the dais and collapsed on the throne with a loud sigh.

"Where is the boy?" he grumbled. "I am too hot."

A guard gestured and a boy of about ten years rushed forward to wave an ostrich feather fan at Pharaoh. Serving women — one of whom I recognised from the dining chamber — came with trays of drinks and sustenance and we waited while he refreshed himself. Sweat trickled behind my knees and I became acutely aware of the dryness of my own mouth as I watched.

It was only once Pharaoh had drunk and eaten his fill that he finally looked out at the waiting women. I straightened my back and held my head high, wondering if he might notice me. After all, surely he knew most of the women here already. Wouldn't he notice the newest addition?

"My beloved subjects," he said. "I have come today to tell you that everything occurs exactly as I have planned. The sun defeats the evil serpent Apophis and rises victorious in the morning because of me. The Great River floods at the right time and to the right height because of me. You have safety and security because of me. I, your great and wise Pharaoh, control everything that happens in the Two Lands. Everything that is good and right is because of me. The Two Lands are great because of me."

He thumped himself on the chest and beamed. This was the man Father had sent me to marry? This self-important, pompous fellow? Surely there were more important things for him to tell us about. Like what was being done to find Nebtu and all the other women who had gone missing. He said our safety and security was because of him? Maybe he didn't even know about Nebtu. Surely he wouldn't sit there in front of us and say such things if he did.

The women around me all nodded and smiled. Every now and then, someone would call out an agreement and others would clap or cheer. Was that really what they thought of Pharaoh's speech? A few rows ahead of me in the prime position at the front was Tiye. Like everyone else, she smiled and clapped and nodded as Pharaoh continued to take credit for everything that was as it should be.

"My lady." Ettu leaned close to whisper in my ear. "You should at least pretend to feel the same enthusiasm as everyone else."

"Can you believe this?" I muttered to her.

"He is Pharaoh and the people here see him as a living god. Whatever your personal opinion might be, you should pretend to think the same."

She was right. I mustered the enthusiasm to plaster a weak smile on my face and the next time everyone else clapped, I did too.

"That's better," Ettu said. "You cannot afford to stick out right now."

Pharaoh droned on and on about his own greatness. The sun crawled all the way across the sky and began its descent to the horizon. The pillar I leaned against provided scant shade, certainly not enough to make up for the heat it gave off. My feet ached, sweat dripped from every limb, and my cheeks were sore from smiling so hard.

A sudden burst of cheers and applause drew me from my thoughts and I realised he had finally finished. I straightened my gown and wiped my sweaty palms on my skirt. Now, surely, he would call for me.

But Pharaoh left, surrounded by his guards. The half-naked women filed after them. A door at the back of the courtyard opened and I could see the waiting palanquin. I watched as he stepped in and the slaves lifted it up onto their shoulders.

Then he was gone. This was the man my father had sent me

halfway around the world to marry and he wasn't even interested in meeting me.

Oh Father, I whispered. *What have you done?*

* * *

Kassaya's journey continues in
Book 2: *Ornament of Pharaoh*

AUTHOR'S NOTE

The story of a foreign princess sent to Egypt with the expectation of being queen, only to discover she won't be, is one I've wanted to tell for a long time. I've also long been intrigued by the events that ended the reign of Ramses III, who is one of perhaps no more than two or three pharaohs who were assassinated (or *probably* assassinated — as with so many things in ancient history, there are no certainties). Given Ramses had a mystery queen — Queen X — who we know absolutely nothing about, this seemed like a prime opportunity to combine the two stories I wanted to tell.

I've often wondered how the women who were shipped off to Pharaoh coped with their situation. Did they know they were going to be one of many hundreds, or even thousands, of "wives"? How many expected, like Kassaya, to be queen? To rule side-by-side with Pharaoh? How did they cope when they discovered the reality of the situation they had been sent to?

The harem inhabitants weren't just those who were sent to Pharaoh by their families either. They also included women captured as spoils of war. Amenhotep II had more than 600 women stolen from Palestine alone, more than half of whom were princesses. So Pharaoh's harem would have comprised a mix of royalty, nobles and peasants. Those who were sent by their families, perhaps some who came willingly, and a lot of women who had been stolen or kidnapped, and didn't want to be there at all. And, of course, the women sent by their families would have brought attendants with them, in some cases, hundreds of them. The palace or palaces that housed all these women, along with the servants who attended to them, must have been truly enormous.

Many of the characters we'll meet in this series have names and occupations drawn from the court records of people who were convicted in the trials following the attack on Ramses III. Most of the male characters are based on people who actually participated in these events. Unfortunately, we don't know the names of the Ornaments involved. For some reason unknown to us, their names were mostly withheld from the court records. However, Ramses did have a secondary wife called Tiye and he had the mysterious Queen X.

The characters of Tall and Half are entirely fictional. I wanted Kassaya to have companions who would be considered outsiders in this time period, people who would be shunned and largely ignored at court. I'm very fond of both Tall and Half, and I'm looking forward to learning more about both of them as the series progresses.

Kylie Quillinan

June 2023

See kyliequillinan.com for more books, including exclusive collections, and newsletter sign up.

ABOUT THE AUTHOR

Kylie writes about women who defy society's expectations. Her novels are for readers who like fantasy with a basis in history or mythology. Her interests include Dr Who, jellyfish and cocktails. She needs to get fit before the zombies come.

Swan – the epilogue to the Tales of Silver Downs series – is available exclusively to her newsletter subscribers. Sign up at kyliequillinan.com.

9 781922 852199